Henry Demarest Lloyd

A Strike of Millionaires Against Miners

The Story of Spring Valley

Henry Demarest Lloyd

A Strike of Millionaires Against Miners
The Story of Spring Valley

ISBN/EAN: 9783337366469

Printed in Europe, USA, Canada, Australia, Japan

Cover: Foto ©Andreas Hilbeck / pixelio.de

More available books at **www.hansebooks.com**

"OUR BAD WEALTH" SERIES, No. 1.

"It is high time OUR BAD WEALTH came to an end."—*Emerson.*

A STRIKE OF MILLIONAIRES

AGAINST MINERS

OR

THE STORY OF SPRING VALLEY

An Open Letter to the Millionaires

BY

HENRY D. LLOYD

CHICAGO:
BELFORD-CLARKE CO., PUBLISHERS
1890

CONTENTS.

A STRIKE OF MILLIONAIRES.

CHAPTER I.

THE PRELUDE OF STARVED ROCK.

WHERE the Illinois sweeps its placid way to the Mississippi between the wooded bluffs of La Salle, and over the sandstone which makes many a picturesque shelf in the valley, stands Starved Rock.

Rising straight from the water-side 125 feet, it can be ascended only by a narrow winding path from the shore. Like one of the mediæval castles which of old threatened but now adorn the lochs of Scotland, Starved Rock once pushed forth from all surroundings, proud of itself as a sure refuge and defense. To-day none but associations of ruin and defeat are intertwined with the beauty of its crumbling head. A fairer scene cannot be than that which lies rolled out before those who clamber to the top — the river, " winding at its own sweet will;" its sedgy banks, the green and yellow grasses of the bottoms that stretch along; the older banks of rock and bluffs a mile apart, which mark where the mightier river flowed in prehistoric days, when the great lakes gave their waters to the Mississippi instead of the St. Lawrence. Farther yet, on the higher level of these older banks, swells away the upland of farm and village and forest. Up the river are Ottawa, Utica, Joliet and scores of other flourishing towns; down the river are La Salle, Peru, and around the bend, out of sight, is Spring Valley, once called the " Magic City," more likely to be known henceforth as the " Tragic City," and to share with Starved Rock the romantic interest of this unhappy happy valley.

The Iroquois, mighty warriors of the Alleghanies, unavailingly fighting east to keep from going west under the compulsion of the stronger race that has always been going west, found themselves crowded into this fair land on an unknown day in some unknown year centuries ago. It was the hunting ground and living ground of a band of the Illinois, a gentler people than the savage Iroquois; but, as the whites had done to the Iroquois, so the Iroquois did to the Illinois. Go west! The last days of these Illinois rose upon them gathered —

a remnant of one hundred men, women and children — on the ample summit of the rock, which rises as a natural castle from the edge of the water. There was room enough for them, and there was timber for their fires. From the broad river a hundred sheer feet and more below no surprise or attack was possible; the narrow pass upward on the side of the land was a Thermopylæ, where a handful could defy a host. There the Illinois stood their last, the Iroquois gathered about. When the besieged lowered their cups for water the strings were cut; when they stole forth for food, they never came back. The river of love in sky, leaf and view, breeze and bird song, which, like the rippling river of water, flowed through the day, flowed in vain before the cruel Iroquois. A few demoniac days of wrath and agony, and the Iroquois stood upon the wide top of the castle of rock, and there were no Illinois—except the dead. It was war, and, to the savage, war was right; but even his heart felt something out of the ordinary in the victory. It had been won, not by hand-to-hand encounter, nor by brave assault, but through the use, day after day, of an advantage of position to deny food and water to a competitor for the possession of land and home.

With a touch of poetry, and perhaps a glimmer of remorse, the Indians, as they told the story, called the place Starved Rock, and Starved Rock the towered fastness will always be. This was War.   War paused here long enough to give this cruel name to the shapely tower, garlanded with green, and then left the valley of the Illinois.   Business came, and Business hath its victories no less renowned than War. At starved Spring Valley, near by, the story of a victory of Business is printed in the same ghastly figures as that in which the Iroquois found their success recorded the morning when, no one opposing, they gained the top of Starved Rock.

CHAPTER II.

ONLY A MODERN INSTANCE.

GREAT difficulties block the way of the thorough investigation of the facts of any particular case of the social problem by persons as ordinarily circumstanced, even when like you to whom these pages are addressed they are stockholders, and, unlike you, are trying to find out what their own directors are doing. It is hoped that this communication — a part of which was first printed in the Chicago *Daily Herald*—may be of service not only to you to whom it is specially addressed, " accessories before and after the fact " of Spring Valley, but to all who want to understand the " works and days " of their brothers and sisters. It was agreed at the National Convention of the American Federation of Labor in Boston, in 1889, that, as their secretary put it, " Miners were worse off than any other workmen in the country." This gives these results of several months' almost constant study of their lot, at a place given world-wide celebrity by their suffering in a peculiarly interesting crisis, some special value. From one learn all. You cannot go over this ground and not gain some insight into the general condition of American labor, and its rela·tions to capital, which were but given at Spring Valley a little more light than usually falls upon them.

I have selected the story of Spring Valley for narration because I have come to know it; not because there has been anything there in your conduct as capitalists and corporations specially worse than what has been done elsewhere. On the contrary, I believe, from my investigations, that the case of Spring Valley is fairly representative of the relations between miners and mine-owners throughout the country — and that is the worst feature of it all. If Spring Valley were exceptional, we could dismiss it as a mere aberration of the commercial conscience of some particularly depraved pot-hunter, and let it go. But when, by reading official documents like the reports of the Ohio legislative committee of 1885 on the Hocking Valley strike, the report of the congressional committee of 1887 on the coal strikes in Pennsylvania, and other authorities, we come to realize that Spring Valley is but one case out of a multitude — but one pustule of a disease spread through the whole body — we begin to get an idea of the seriousness of our social condition.

The story of Spring Valley needs but a change of names and a few details to be the story of Braidwood, Ill., where babies and men and women wither away to be transmigrated into the dividends of a millionaire coalminer of Beacon street, Boston. It needs but a few changes to be the story of Punxsutawney — where starving foreigners have eaten up all the dogs in the country to keep themselves loyally alive to dig coal again when their masters re-open the coal kennels; and Scranton, and the Lehigh Valley, where the hard, very hard coal barons of Pennsylvania manufacture artificial winter for twelve months of every year. It needs but a few changes to be the story of Brazil, Ind., where the Brazil Block Coal Company locked out their thousands of miners last year until their wives and children grew transparent enough to be glasses through which the miners could read, though darkly, the terms of surrender which they had to accept. It needs but a few changes to be the story of the Hocking Valley, where Pinkerton gunpowder was burned to give the light by which Labor could read " the free contract " its brother Capital wanted it to sign — or the story of the Reading collieries, where, as the congressional committee of 1887–1888 reported, the employer provoked the miners to riot, and then shot the rioters " legally." The story of Spring Valley needs not many changes to be a picture of what all American industry will come to be if the power of our Bourbons of business, such as you have shown yourselves to be at Spring Valley, develops at its present rate up to the end of the nineteenth century.

CHAPTER III.

WHO HATH DONE THIS THING ?

FOUR legal dummies, or fictitious "persons," were the creators of Spring Valley. These were the four corporations, the Chicago & North-Western Railroad, the Spring Valley Coal Company, the Spring Valley Town Site Company, and the Northwest Fuel Company of St. Paul, behind which you who were the real persons are masked. According to any right standard of morals and law, every one of you who is a stockholder in those corporations must bear his share of the responsibility for what was done, just as each of you gladly receives his share of the profits. At the beginning, Spring Valley and its miseries and wrongs were the conception and achievement of but one or two among the leading owners of the railroad and the other companies. These few did the planning, secured the approval of the board of directors, and the active officers of the railroad, let in "on the ground floor" the influential men whose help they wanted, got

the special freight rates needed to enable the
" enterprise" to steal the business of its competitors, bought the coal land, and invented the
various details of the scheme by which fortunes
for you and themselves were to be made out
of the public need for coal, the workingmen's
need for employment, and the misuse of the
powers of the common carrier. At the incep-
tion of the " enterprise," as Ali Baba would
have us call it, some of the directors and most
of the stockholders of the railroad, if not those
of the other corporations, could plead that
they had no actual knowledge of what was going on, and so no real responsibility for it.
But the press and other indignant protestants
when the iniquities of years culminated in the
" lock-out" made the whole matter, ending in
this strike of the millionaires against the miners,
a common scandal.   But so far as the public
know, not one of you, the directors, not
one of you, the stockholders, in whose name
and for whose profit the campaign of starvation
and slander was carried on, has disavowed or discouraged it.   You all seem to have accepted
unprotestingly your share of the guilt — and
gilt; and, if you have had any other anxiety
than that the millionaires should succeed in their
strike against the miners so that you might have

more gilt, you have never let the public become aware of it. Not one of you, so far as known, sent a word of sympathy, or a mouthful of food, to the thousands who were being ground to powder by your agents for your benefit. Just who you are, accessories of the original willing sinners, the people cannot learn, for the names of the stockholders of our public corporations are kept in closest secrecy as one of the prerogatives of the private ownership of public highways. The laws of the State of Illinois require its railroads to keep records in Chicago, in which the transfers of stock are noted. Even that is not done by these bundles of men — so powerful because so well tied together. They think it of no ill omen to themselves, who get their vast wealth from control of the roads, given them by the law, to set a public example of flagrant nullification of law. The corporation, which the great political economist Adam Smith predicted would never come into general use, has grown to be the almost universal instrument of modern business. It has become greater than government, and it shrouds its members in a secrecy, under the dark protection of which they can, with impunity, give rein to passions of power and greed. They have the cloak of invisibility, and they use it as men of prey and lust would use the darkness of our streets if cities put out their lights and went back to mediaeval gloom and crime. The public cannot penetrate into the anonymity which protects all of you who are responsible for Spring Valley. It only knows the names of those who were your " directors," among whom are the largest owners, or representatives of the largest owners, but does not know what part they may have taken in the transactions described in this book, nor to what degree their responsibility is actual or constructive. This is as lucky for those actually guilty, who are lost in the crowd, as it is unlucky for those who are discredited by being associated with them. For the Chicago & North-Western Railway the directors were : Messrs. Albert Keep, Chauncey M. Depew, N. K. Fairbank, William K. Vanderbilt, F. W. Vanderbilt, John I. Blair, William L. Scott, Marvin Hughitt, Horace Williams, John M. Burke, H. M. Twombley, D. O. Mills, Samuel F. Barger, Percy R. Pyne, A. G. Dulman, M. L. Sykes, D. P. Kimball, and for the Town Site Company, the Coal Company, and the Northwest Fuel Co. of St. Paul, Messrs. Scott, Saunders, and Sheppard, among others. The Spring Val-

ley Coal Company, owning and mining the coal
lands ; the Town Site Company, buying farms
to sell as " city lots," were organized and are
owned and controlled by a powerful interest
—powerful both in ownership and authority
—in the Chicago & North-Western Railroad.
The same interest reappears in part in the
Northwest Fuel Company, of St. Paul.   In
the annual report which you who own the
North-Western Railroad made to the stockholders and the public for the fiscal year ending May 31, 1885, you said: " The company
has found it necessary to begin the construction of about seventy-five miles of railroad,
projected as a coal road, under the charter of
the Northern Illinois Railway, extending from
the coal deposits adjacent to La Salle, Ill., to
Belvidere, on the Freeport line, where it forms
a direct connection with the lines of this company, for the distribution of coal in the State
of Wisconsin and throughout the Northwest.
The lines will be a great local convenience to
the company in reaching a supply of fuel by
the shortest and cheapest route for its own
consumption and for the wants of the general
public.   The means for its construction are
procured by the issue and sale of the Northern
Illinois first mortgage five per cent. twenty-

2

five year bonds at the rate of $20,000 a mile
for seventy-five miles, and the bonds are guar-
anteed, principal and interest, by the Chicago
& North-Western Railroad, the sole owners of
the property." This announcement the public
afterward saw was made good by the expenditure of large sums — $207,802.82 in 1884–5,
$1,120,177.47 in 1885–6, $72,112.78 in 1886–7.

The owners of the North-Western Railroad
and the coal company, in part the same persons, made contracts with each other, that is
themselves, for the purchase of the coal and
for the rates at which it should be moved.
Whenever the question of coal freights between
northern Illinois and the Northwest was dis-
cussed by any meeting of traffic managers,
those representing the owners of the North-
Western road always made a fight to get the
best rates for the North-Western's coal from
Spring Valley. The road made the same
charge for the Western trade for hauling coal
from Spring Valley as from Chicago; that is,
it hauled the coal from Spring Valley to Chicago for nothing. By the powerful help of the
managers of the road the product of Spring
Valley has made its appearance at all the important coal-buying points in the Northwest
at prices which made it morally certain to the

unhappy competitors that its shippers got a rebate. Numberless circumstances have indicated so close a relation between the railroad
and the coal company that the latter is habitu-
ally spoken of in the trade as the " North-
Western's coal mine," and always so among
railroad men.

A common personality runs through the
ownership of the railroad, the coal mine, the
town lots, and the fuel company's business.
Through this mutual element an identity of
interest was established for all the associated
capitalists of these enterprises, who represent
upward of $500,000,000 at the least. The
identity of interest has been practical, not
nominal. They have accepted the results, still
possess them, and are expectantly waiting for
more. Through the easy machinery of the corporation, which is your kind of labor union, there
has been a concert of action, with a common
design, for a common object. The profits on
the sale of farms as city lots to laborers and
tradesmen, on the transportation of the coal,
on the use of it for the locomotives of the
road, on the buying and selling of it, on the
sales of supplies to the miners, have gone
to one or another of you to whom this letter
is addressed. You cannot share in the benefits

of this co-operation without sharing its responsibilities, even though you act through the con-
venient impersonality of the corporation.   You
are the " Captains of Industry " in this enterprise,
and, if you accept the acts of your agents, they
are your acts.   Your agent has appealed in
numbers of public statements to the public to
be the arbiter between you and the workingmen
and business men of Spring Valley, whose
harm he has wrought — and you have wrought
if you abide with him — for your business
gain.   " With public opinion," said Lincoln,
" all things are possible; against it, nothing is
possible."   Whether your agent has done
wisely to appeal to public opinion depends
altogether upon whether the things done for
you to the men he and you have persuaded to
dig your coal, buy your goods and real estate,
and accept the " good chance for a home " you
advertised, have been fair and square, kindly
and honest.   There has been a profit on all
the various branches of the enterprise.   The
company store and the land speculation have
made money.   The railroad has reduced the
cost of fuel for its locomotives, and the coal
company has added to its plant out of its
profits, though it has made no dividend.   But
whether your attempt to make money has been

successful or not makes here not one iota of difference.   Public opinion has not yet rotted down to the point of permitting rich men, men skilled in affairs, to violate all their pledges to poor and inexperienced followers, simply because profits have been unsatisfactory, nor will it allow the capitalist to starve the laborer to make larger profits.

CHAPTER IV.

BOOMING THE TOWN.

You in your different provinces created this enterprise, with its railroad, coal mines, land speculation and fuel business in 1884, acting simultaneously and re-enforcing each other. Where Spring Valley is, there was then only field and forest. The land you needed had to be obtained from the farmer. You gave them $35 up to $80 an acre, in very few cases more, for land which you resold in lots for thousands of dollars an acre. Where you bought only the right to the coal underneath you paid them sometimes less than $10 an acre, seldom much more, for rights for which $15 to $35 an acre is gladly paid in neighboring localities by other companies.

Town site companies are a familiar device in the development of the money-making possibilities of the modern railroad man. They are all about the same thing. They are made up by insiders in railroad management. These insiders take advantage of their knowledge as

to where new lines are to be built and where
the railroads mean to stop their trains, or they
use their power to say where they shall stop.
Knowing the one or commanding the other,
they buy up the land of the farmers who do not
know it, at prices far below their prospective
value. These farms, converted into cities, on
paper, and sliced up into diminutive metro-
politan lots, are then sold to credulous people
at fictitious prices created by every artifice of
advertising, of wash sales, of mushroom prosperity produced by all the means within the
power of railroad manipulations. When the
game of "terminal points," "new hotels,"
"great manufacturing center," "car-shop site,"
"grand opera house," "investments by the
directors themselves," has been worked for all
it is worth at one point, the great men move on
to the next town, to repeat the same process.

While shrewd agents busied themselves in
buying up the lands of uninformed farmers,
maps were made of the "city" of Spring
Valley, by the Town Site Company, whose
only "improvements" consisted in laying off
the new metropolis on paper. All the making of roads, lighting, grading, sidewalking,
and other needed work were left to be made
by the purchasers of its lots, when they

wanted to use them. Those of you who established the Spring Valley Town Site Company gerrymandered its boundaries so that your coal mines, advertised by you to be the "principal industry " of the town, lay outside the town.

You thereby escaped your share of municipal taxation, and threw it on the workingmen and the tradesmen, who gave your property all its value.

How did you of the coal company and the land company sell this land, and how did you draw in the workingmen and others to dig your coal and buy your real estate? In the first number of the Spring Valley *Gazette* you published the following advertisement. It covered half a page with the biggest kind of black type, and ran with changes as needed in the paper for nearly four years until the middle of May, 1889. The date of the following is November 14, 1885:

A CHANCE
For making
Profitable investments
In the town of
Spring Valley, situated in the eastern part of Bureau County,
on the line of Chicago, Rock Island & Pacific Railway
and the terminus of the Chicago and North-
Western Railroad, offers extraordinary
inducements to every one who
may desire

A GOOD LOCATION
FOR
BUSINESS OR A HOME.
The principal industry upon which the town is now dependent
is its
IMMENSE COAL FIELDS,
Comprising about fifteen thousand acres, which are being
rapidly developed by the Spring Valley Coal Company.
Three mines are already in operation.
Within eighteen months at least
TWO THOUSAND
MINERS WILL FIND
STEADY EMPLOYMENT.
The bright prospects for the place shortly becoming one of the
leading manufacturing towns in the State, with
Good drainage,
Plenty of good water,
Excellent building stone,
Brick yards, etc., and with the two lines of railroad to Chicago
and Milwaukee, and surrounded by one of the best
farming districts in the State offers to all
who may
DESIRE A CHANGE IN LOCATION OF BUSINESS
A chance seldom found.
Building and business lots are offered at
LOW PRICES.
TERMS REASONABLE.
For further information, write or apply to the Vice-President
and General Manager Spring Valley Coal Company,
Spring Valley, Ill.

This advertisement and similar ones were
circulated all over the country in newspapers
and pamphlets. When it became known that
you, who owned the North-Western Railroad,
were to extend its tracks to Spring Valley, the

miners who had hesitated to sell their homes elsewhere and move in, the little capitalists in surrounding towns who had hesitated to invest their savings in the purchase of lots, hesitated no longer. Where such men led, it was safe for them to follow, and they followed. ⁕

The Spring Valley *Gazette* of November 14, 1885, said: "What makes Spring Valley different from other coal towns is the fact that the contracts for the coal were made before the fields were open. It is to supply the Chicago & North-Western and the vast coal-using country tributary to that system. The coal company is the largest soft-coal corporation in the country, having a paid-up capital of $1,500,000. The selling of lots began in July last, and at the present time (July to November) about 1,000 lots have been sold. The price of lots ranges from $150 to $300." According to these figures, which were probably furnished to the *Gazette* by the agent of the town-site company to help the "boom," the total sales in the first six months had been about $200,000 for land which had cost less than $20,000.

From the coal-mining places in Illinois and the neighboring States miners who could move did so. It was by the best of their class that the skillfully prepared bait was taken. It was not the lazy miners who took the trouble to move themselves to the new industrial center. It was not the poor workers who could not get out of debt where they were — it was not the thoughtless and intemperate, who had saved no money with which to make the transfer. The men who came to Spring Valley were picked men — selected out of the whole number of the coal miners of the country by their intelligence, their thrift, their habits of industry. These men read the statements published by the Chicago & North-Western Railway, the Spring Valley Coal Company and the Town Site Company, and, seeing that the leaders of the enterprise were of the best business talent of America, and able, with their hundreds of millions of capital, to carry out any enterprise they undertook, decided, without a second thought, "Spring Valley is the place for us and our families." From Streator, La Salle, Braidwood, Peru, from all the neighboring coal-mining towns, miners who had saved money enough to buy homes for themselves sold them, and bought lots, went to work, and began to build in Spring Valley to get the greater advantages promised by the greater capital, better equipments and more skillful management of the "captains of industry" there. The announcements and advertisements of these rich and powerful and experienced men of affairs assured them of steady work, living wages, and all the appliances of civilization. It was not miners alone who were taken in the net. Traders in every line of business in the surrounding towns sold out, and reinvested in Spring Valley.

Paragraphs like these, culled from the local press, give a hint of the fervor with which your lead was followed:

The Joliet *Record*, in February, 1886, said: " In Spring Valley there are now three hundred voters where six months ago were only a few farms. One hundred thousand dollars have since that time been invested there in business houses, residences and tenements."

The Spring Valley *Gazette* said, on March 27, 1886: " No less than twelve new buildings were begun this week." April 10th: " Spring Valley is booming." April 17th: " From the *Gazette* office sixteen new buildings can be seen in construction. Talk about ' boom;' the word is tame and feeble to express the activity of Spring Valley." April 10th: " Mr. and Mrs. Fleming, of Sheffield, were in our city this week and purchased several lots." April

26th: "One of Streator's heaviest capitalists has $7,000 invested in Spring Valley real estate." On October, 1888, the *Gazette* said: "On Wednesday a number of Eastern capitalists, accompanied by Marvin Hughitt, general manager of the North-Western Railroad, were in town, and were so favorably impressed with the 'Magic City' that they intend to put some money in it. Let her boom."

How successful the boomers were the triumphant changes in the advertisements in the pamphlets, papers, etc., show. A few months after the appearance of the advertisement given above a new one was prepared and took its place. This was circulated broadcast in the newspapers, filling a half page in the Spring Valley *Gazette*, and also in a pamphlet specially prepared to boom the town, and distributed for that purpose throughout the country. Here is the new advertisement:

"SPRING VALLEY."

The coming manufacturing town of the State of Illinois, situated in Bureau County, at the terminus of the Chicago & North-Western Railway, and on the lines of the C., R. I. & P. and Burlington Railway.

The principal industry upon which the town is dependent are its immense coal fields, comprising 40,000 acres and five large mines already sunk, which are being developed by the Spring Valley Coal Company.

LARGE INDUCEMENTS TO MANUFACTURERS—
—GOOD LOCATION FOR A HOME.

Other large mines in the vicinity of Spring Valley are also in operation. The town has now a population of 4,500, and is rapidly increasing.

2,000 men are now employed in the mines of the Spring Valley Coal Co., and in less than two years will employ from 3,500 to 4,000 men.

BUILDING AND BUSINESS LOTS AT LOW PRICES,

AND ON THE MOST REASONABLE TERMS.

The Good Drainage, Plenty of Water, Excellent Building
Stone, Brick Yards, Etc., together with the Three
Lines of Railway to Chicago and Milwaukee,
and surrounded with one of the best
farming districts in the State,
makes it a most desirable
place to locate.

——————

For further information or particulars, address
the Vice-President and Gen. Manager
Spring Valley Coal Co., Spring Valley, Bureau Co., Ill.

The changes are significant. The coal fields, which at first covered only 15,000 acres, now amount to 40,000. The coal had proved so good and the operations of the mines so satisfactory that 25,000 acres more of coal rights had been purchased. The population, which had been too small to mention in the first advertisement, had now grown to 4,500, " and is rapidly increasing." The three mines have become five. The prophecy that " within eighteen months at least two thousand miners will find steady employment " has been verified, and the new prophecy is put out that " in less than two years the mines will employ from 3,500 to 4,000 men."

There were many ways of luring into this paradise the workmen without the sweat of whose brows you could not eat bread. There have been all through the summer of 1889 hundreds of Belgian and French women and children and a few men in Spring Valley who have been kept from starvation only by kinder hearts than their employers, and who were enticed thither from their homes and employment in France and Belgium by false representations made by an agent whose foot-tracks his victims declare they have traced straight to the company's office in Spring Valley. In the Pittsburg *Labor Tribune* of September 28, 1886, we read: " Parties from Spring Valley were in Decatur last week looking for 200 men to go to work there." The advertisements in newspapers and pamphlets circulated everywhere drew men from points as far away as Iowa and Colorado to get " steady employment" and a " good chance for a home."

These tactics of your agent, in befooling, with false promises, honest and sturdy foreign workingmen to come over to flood the labor market of Spring Valley, are unfortunately no new thing in American " business " methods, but they are all the worse for being old. The "supply" of labor is in this way made to over-run the "demand," and the sacred character of the "immutable law of supply and demand" is given an illustration which working-men understand, even if political economists do not. The "unchanging" law, when worked in this way, increases the number of the customers who buy goods at the "pluck-me" stores kept by the company, makes wages low by the underbidding of the unemployed against the employed; it keeps the men poor, humble, and submissive to all your regulations and exactions. This method of regulating "supply and demand" is not a native product of Illinois. It is an importation from Pennsylvania. The select committee of Congress which investigated the labor troubles in Pennsylvania in 1888, say:

"Many thousands of surplus laborers are always kept on hand to underbid each other for employment, and thereby force the men to submit to whatever treatment the company may impose. Squads of Poles, Italians, and Huns, many of whom cannot speak English, throng the mines to compete for work. *

* * * The question will force itself, Why are the mines overrun by these foreigners?

How do they get there? and by whose agency?"

I visited many of these French and Belgians. As a rule, only the women and children were at home. The men had gone away to seek work in other towns, and even in other States. Very poor the homes were, and gaunt the women and children. Clothing, food, bedding, furniture, were all down to the lowest level of a pitiful minimum. How had they happened to come to America? A man had come to them at Pas-de-Calais, and Courcelles-les-Sens, etc., etc., and told them of the good pay and the good times they could have at Spring Valley.

" He gave us a card, and, if we gave that to the gentleman at Spring Valley, he would give us the good work and the high wages."

" Were they glad they had come? "

" Oh, monsieur, see how we live. It was better at home! If we could only get back. We did better at home."

I listened. Of course, there would be angry words, vindictive outbreaks of indignation against those who had so cruelly unhomed and expatriated them for the sake of a little extra profit. But there was nothing of the kind, not even a flash of wrath. The poor people

3

answered all inquiries gently and patiently and intelligently, but never a harsh word against their oppressors. They even laughed as they talked. It was as if they felt it all to be part of the inevitable ill fortune of life, which they must bear as best they could. I was amazed and humbled. It seemed to me that, had I been thus made the victim of inhuman greed for " more," had I and my home and my life been butchered—not " to make a Roman holiday," but an American dividend —I would have thought a lifetime too little to give to a crusade of retribution. The truth then first really dawned upon me, that there is a sanctification which comes, however unconsciously, to the victims of wrong and injustice, and that it is the master, not the slave, who receives the double curse of oppres sion.

It was a brilliant success, this booming of the town, and great was the profit of it. A more brilliant stroke still was to follow, and greater would be the profit of that, the dooming of the town.

Those were bright days in Spring Valley, in 1885, 1886, 1887, when the soft notes of the " boomer " called every one to " profitable investments," " steady employment," " good

chances for a home," and " special inducements
to business." People of all kinds were pour-
ing into the magic city. The Rev. John F.
Powers, in charge of a well-established Catholic church at Peru, gave it up, and came to
Spring Valley to build up a new congregation.
Other clergymen and doctors and teachers
came, and workingmen of all kinds. Rents
were high, buildings could be rented for $180
a month that cost only $3,000 to build. Those
who bought lots could turn around immediately and sell them at a handsome advance.
The miners, under the promise of steady employment, bought your lots on monthly payments, and began to build homes, getting their
lumber and material of the company. The
miners had to buy their lots under arrangements which forfeited all they had paid, and
the lot, too, if at any time they discontinued
their monthly payments, no matter how near
the end of their indebtedness they might have
got. This forfeiture could be declared by the
company without notice to the poor miner,
and without any legal proceedings in which he
might defend his rights. But the miners were
brave-hearted; they loved to have homes of
their own, and they made these razor-edged
agreements and went in debt for lumber, be-

lieving all would come out right, since there
was to be " steady employment."

Upon inquiring among these trusting men
for copies of the deeds or contracts executed
between the seller and these simple-minded buyers, I cannot find any.   But I do find cases in
which the company sold lots without giving the
workingman who bought a shred of title to
attest their rights.   Taking sometimes 33 per
cent. of the price in cash, it charged them with
the balance, and took part of their pay every
month to wipe it off.   All that such buyers
had to show for their money and title were a
receipt and an entry on the books, and what
is an entry worth when it is in the books of
men who deal thus with poor and inexperienced " brothers"?   Not one of you would
buy ten cents' worth of land in that way.

There were, at last, five thousand people in
Spring Valley; the main business street had
two rows of flourishing stores; there were two
places of worship, a public library and gym-
nasium, clubs and debating societies, Knights
of Labor assemblies, a court-room, two hotels,
and an opera house.   Very intelligent men
the miners were — the picked men of the
industry.   There were not a few among them
who could discuss the theories of Henry

George, Herbert Spencer, Darwin, with any one. Strangers who visited the clubs and debating societies of the miners declared themselves astonished by their intelligence and range of knowledge. These were days of hope and growth. One cloud there was. The miners, work their hardest, could not make the wages they had been promised. The mines were good, and of a kind miners liked to work in, for they were free from water, and no powder was required. But the earnings of the men were barely enough to carry them through. A man in a good place, with steady work, could earn $45 to $60 in a month, and more if he got into a particularly good " pocket," but work was never continuous. Sometimes it was a fall of rock in the roadway; sometimes a lack of cars to take away the coal; sometimes a suspension on account of a dull market; sometimes a man's room or place in the vein would be shut off by a new road, and he would have to wait until another place could be had. Sometimes it was one thing, sometimes another; but the upshot of it was that, mostly, when the miner came to settle with the company for the preceding month's work, he found that, after, paying for his oil, and the sharpening of his tools, his rent or his monthly installment on the lot he had bought, his monthly contribution to the doctor, and his bill at the company's store, there was nothing left. He had just made ends meet; perhaps he was a little behind. Take it by the year, doing well one month, idle the whole of the next, the men could not make much more than about $30 a month. That is to say, they got for their lives and labor a scanty allowance of food, clothing, roofing, but not enough; and practically nothing of the many other things which people must have who are to keep up their health and strength — nothing for their old age, and nothing to help them for their duties as fathers and citizens.

The physical conditions under which the Spring Valley miners work are better than those in many other places, but they are not easy. You for whom the coal is dug, either for your dividends or your comfort, as you sit before your glowing fires, are too far away from the toil and trouble of the miner. They spend ten hours a day in their caverns — pitch dark — except for the flicker and glimmer of the little lamp each carries in the front of his cap. For months in the short winter days, when it is not yet light at seven, and is dark by half-past five, these men see daylight, only

on Sunday — once a week. They have to work
upon their knees, or lying on their side, or
stooping low, and sometimes are obliged to lie
flat on their backs while digging at the ceil-
ing.

This hard work in a room three feet or three
feet six inches high, hundreds of feet below the
surface, in the gloom of perpetual night, with air
to breathe got only by artificial and imperfect
ventilation, is the human price that has to be
paid on all our coal. You know this coal only
as light, heat, power, profit, comfort, a means
of longer life or greater wealth. To the miner
it is a black and obdurate enemy, a jailer that
imprisons him, shutting out his sunlight, the
fresh air of the hills and meadows, the sounds
of birds and the river; threatening him daily
with death or mutilation in strange and terrible forms, and rewarding his faithfulest and
luckiest toil with less than the cost of subsistence — if the cost of subsistence of the American citizen of this free and glorious republic, is
to include food, clothing, shelter, family life,
amusement, education, leisure, and old age.

Such subsistence as this is possible to no
miner, and becomes more impossible every
day. It is easy for the owner of the mines,
the stockholders, to juggle with their figures

of capital, operating expenses, profit and loss,
to convince the public that they cannot pay
living wages. The poorest of these stockholders lives in a social world which to the
miner would seem a heaven. The contrast
between their " much," and the miner's " little,"
puts all their bookkeeping to the blush. It is
this gulf between the lot of the employer and
that of the employé, all through our modern life which gives its pulse to the social question. A llthe bookkeeping in the world cannot write out the deficit which the workingmen's account shows in comparison with that
of the business men. In every city, the contrast between what is got by the brothers who
employ and the brothers who are employed,
speaks for itself.

None of the promises of steady employment
and good pay were fulfilled. As to the pay
Messrs. Gould and Wines, the latter secretary
of the State Board of Charities, the special com-
missioner appointed by the governor to investigate the trouble in these and the adjoining
coal regions, reported, August, 1889, after
careful inquiry, that the average was $31.62
per month, which they declared was " certainly
less than any laboring man ought to receive."
Take a concrete case which is worth all the sta-

tistics in the world: C—— W—— is a steady German miner, who has had fifteen years' experience in the mines. He has been at Spring Valley four years. When you gentlemen of $500,000,000 invited him to come to Spring Valley he was working at Coal City. He sold the house and lot he had bought with his savings there, and bought a lot at Spring Valley, paying at the rate of $1,400 an acre for what cost you between $50 and $80 an acre, a profit of about 2,000 per cent. His earnings the first month were $13, and he has been " laid off " by the company for weeks and months at a time. His highest wages for any month in the four years have been $65. I procured his monthly statements of account with the company for the eight months ending with the lock-out in May. His earnings for the entire period were $230.07, an average of $28.76 a month, and of this he actually received only $28.56 in cash, all the rest being taken by the company for supplies bought at the company store. This man was absolutely temperate ; he could not have been very riotous on $28 in eight months. His wife told me that he had never been able to make enough in Spring Valley to support the family, and that she and the eldest daughter had had to go out washing to keep them alive. He has eight children. He was foolish enough, relying on the leadership of the gentlemen to whom this letter is addressed, to build a house, borrowing part of the money. Your lock-out cut off the little income he had. When I saw him his interest was overdue, and he was awaiting in quiet despair a foreclosure which would sweep away all that remained of fifteen years' hard work and savings. Yet this man and his wife told their story without a word, look or tone of the righteous wrath against you which I should have supposed would consume their hearts. How thrifty and good a man C—— W—— is I could see by a little advertisement of his I found in looking over the files of the local paper. It was inserted when he first came to Spring Valley, full of hope, and willing to work at night at home after working all day at the mines. It read: " C—— W—— will receive orders for carpet weaving at his home, —— street."

Against such instances from real life and the careful investigations of the commissioners of the State, it is ridiculous for the coal com.. pany to put forward, as it has done, a statement of the earnings of twenty-five men, picked out of 2,500, as fair specimens of the

way in which the millionaires have divided
with the miners.*

The statements which the company makes
monthly to its men are called "Miner's Ab-
stracts." Here is one of them obtained from
a miner. The man is not designated by his
name, but by a number — in this case 2,103 —
stamped on tin tags, which he puts on all the
loaded cars he sends out of the mine, so that
they may be credited to him. This abstract
needs no explanation. It shows, that, when the
company settled with "No. 2,103" in the
middle of March for the work done in February,
there was no money due him. He had earned
$23.13, which does not seem to be "at the
rate of $2.50 to $4 a day," but it was all
soaked up by the charges the company had
against him for oil, tool-sharpening, fuel, and
the "store." The company owed him $23.13;
he owed the company $23.13. They were
"even," and he had the priceless privilege of

* There is no way of making money out of these poor men too small
for their rich employers. They charged the miners last year a cent a ton
for sharpening their tools. On the annual production of 1,000,000 to
1,500,000 tons, this would yield the company $10,000 to $15,000 for the
services of blacksmiths, who could not cost, with all allowances for fuel,
shops, etc., more than $2,000 altogether. This was a profit of $8,000 to
$12,000 to the company on an investment of $2,000, and their poor men
had to furnish both the investment and the profit! This is an illustration
which will serve to make clear what is meant by "high finance," and why
it is that so many are poor, while a few are so rich. Before going back to
work after the recent lock-out, the men succeeded in getting this charge for
smithy reduced one-half, but they still have to pay the company thousands of dollars a year, besides paying all it costs to sharpen their tools.

delving again into the depths to see if he could keep in that nicely balanced state of impecuniosity, so full of heartening stimulation and encouragement to the free citizen.

MINER'S ABSTRACT.

SPRING VALLEY COAL COMPANY.

Spring Valley, Ill., Mar. 12, '89.

Ck. 2,103.

CR.

Tons 25.14	$23.13
Yds. Entry.	
Days' Labor	
Extra	
	$23.13

DR.

Collections	$0.25
House Rent	
Cash	
Powder	
Tools	
Smithing	0.26
Fuel	3.20
Oil, etc.	
Weighman	0.26
Store	19.16
	$23.13

Sometimes several men work as partners in one room in the mine, and send out their joint product in the same cars and marked with the same number. This number, or " miner's check," as it is called, will in such cases represent the earnings of two or three men. I have before me several such partnership numbers with statements of their earnings for several months. They show amounts of $127, $138, $116, earned by four men; of $47, $60, $65, earned by two men, showing average monthly earnings of $24.33 each. The miners told me that the large earnings reported by the mine-owners as made by some of their men, are shown by representing the amount of one of these partnership checks to be the earnings of one man. At the conference at Joliet in September, 1889, between the miners and mine-owners, under the auspices of the special commission appointed by the governor of Illinois, one of the mine-owners produced a statement of this kind, seeming to prove that his men were making very large earnings. But it happened that some of the men present knew the number, and were able to point out that the earnings paraded as specimens of what a miner could do, were in truth the combined wages of several miners in partnership, and they thus successfully exposed the misrepresentation.

Still, these were days of hope and growth. The miners knew that the opening years of a new mine were not its best; that there were in this, as always in new enterprises, all sorts of hitches, accidents and disappointments. Things would mend, and they could afford to wait, for the advertisements of the coal company promised them " steady employment," and the great and good men who had opened the mines and with others had built the North-Western track to the mines " for a supply of fuel for the road and the West and Northwest tributary to it," were not triflers.

So after all, notwithstanding the trials and disappointments, it was a happy community which began, in December, 1888, to get ready to celebrate Christmas, day of peace on earth, and good will among men.

CHAPTER V.

DOOMING THE TOWN.

THE " boomers " were getting their Christmas present ready for the miners, merchants, parsons, teachers, workingmen, who had added to their millions by coming to Spring Valley.

On a December afternoon, without previous warning, the miners in shafts Nos. 3 and 4 were told to take away their tools at the close of the day, and not return, as that part of the mine would be closed until further notice.

This threw about 700 men, one-third of the working population of the town, out of work for an unknown time at the beginning of winter —men, too, who had been earning only just enough to keep body and soul together, no more.

Without a word of warning! There was no strike, no whisper of strike; the men had been working faithfully, digging the coal according to orders, and taking the pay as agreed.

Thus the gentlemen of many millions sitting under brilliantly illuminated Christmas trees in joyous mansions in Chicago, Erie, St. Paul, New York, by a click of the telegraph make a present of midwinter disemployment to one third of " their " town.

Without notice! This has a familiar look again. It is the Pennsylvania plan, which is being introduced into the industries of the free West. Like the means, some of which have been hinted at, by which the wages of the miners were cut into and cut down, this unannounced stoppage of work is one of the well-worn practices of railroad and coal-mining combinations of Pennsylvania to " break" in the men. The congressional report on the labor troubles in Pennsylvania in 1888 describes this Pennsylvania method. (Page 5.)

" Then, again, as no coal mine can be successfully worked except full-handed — that is, with a full complement of experts and laborers — the railroads, which both mine and carry coal, always retain an abundant supply of help on hand, which help they purposely keep in ignorance as to when operations will be suspended, and for how long. If the knowledge of when they shall be required to work short time or no time were not deliberately withheld from the miners and laborers till the last moment, they would doubtless seek employment elsewhere."

In this way the dooming of the town began, and we will see it unfolding step by step by a perfectly planned scheme, just as clearly as we saw the booming of the town progress by act on act of unerring " commercial sagacity," to the great profit of the " sagacious."

Why the men must quit work, they never knew; why the " steady employment" promised them so disastrously ceased, they were not told.

The Spring Valley *Gazette* giving the news of the shut-down in its issue of January 3d, gave no reason, but spoke of it as " temporary."

Subsequent events have furnished a ghastly commentary on its concluding remark: " It is consoling to hear the more sensible men speak with confidence of the ruling power here in which they have implicit belief."

The generosity of the remainder of the men still at work, induced them to share their work with the unemployed, so that for the rest of the winter three families had to live on the wages that before had not been enough for two. The promise was made by the company, that the suspension of work would be but temporary, and that all should soon have

4

full employment again. The whole population staggered through that winter as best
they could. The company would not give
them work nor help, but it fed them with
words of hope, which kept them from going
elsewhere. The people asked for bread, and
you gave them paragraphs like these:

"The indications are that the output at the
mines will soon be increased."—Spring Valley
Gazette, January 3, 1889.

"All the miners in this city are now having
full work — not full time, of course — but, if the
present kind of weather keeps on, they soon
will have."— Spring Valley *Gazette*, January
10, 1889.

"Spring Valley," said the *Gazette* of Janu-
uary 17th, "is merely taking a little doze, preparatory to big, rushing business next fall," and
on January 24th, "The day is not far distant
when more business will be done in Spring
Valley than was ever before."

April 25, 1889, the *Gazette* announced that
the "Spring Valley Coal Co. had opened a
rail coal yard in Chicago," and that was hailed
by the desperate people as certainly good evidence that "steady employment" was coming
again.

Four days later, the next stroke in the

Dooming of the Town fell. On Monday, April 29th, the men in the mines were told, that, when they quit work for the day, they could take out their tools, as the mines would be closed until further notice. In one afternoon, again without previous notice, all the miners of the town were deprived of their livelihood. They had not struck; they had not asked for any increase in wages; they had made no new demands of any kind upon their employers.* Simultaneously with the closing of the mines, the company's store was closed. The company did not intend that any of its groceries should help to feed, nor any of its woolens warm, the people. No explanation was vouchsafed as to when the mines would be re-opened. The men were simply told to take out their tools at the close of the day, and not come back until they were bid. They were locked out. It was a strike, but it was a strike of millionaires against miners. It was a strike of dollars against men; of dollars which could lie idle one year, two years, longer if

* Report on the Coal-Miners' Strike and Lock-Out in Northern Illinois, by J. M. Gould and Fred. H. Wines, special commissioners appointed by the governor, August, 1889, page 5.
"The present suspension," said the commissioners of the State, "assumes more the form of a strike at Streator and Braidwood, but of a lock-out in the vicinity of La Salle, especially at Spring Valley, where the miners were notified to take their tools out, and have not had any terms offered them on which the company is willing again to employ them."

necessary, and be dollars still, against men
who began to fade into nothingness the next
day.   It was a strike of rich men against poor
men.   It was a strike in violation of every
pledge, tacit and expressed, which these rich
men had given when they built their railroad,
and sold the land, and opened the mines, and
called in the men from other work far and near.
It was a strike which brought woe and want
upon innocent thousands for the sake of extra
profits on stocks and bonds.   To " make more
money," disease and starvation were invited to
come to Spring Valley, and they came.

CHAPTER VI.

THE GHOST OF STARVED ROCK WALKS ABROAD.

THE people who had been digging your coal, buying your lots, supporting your disemployed, making business for your railroad, began to starve at once. The men scattered all over the country in search of work, and the women with their babies took to the roads to beg. Within a month the local papers announced that two-thirds of the men had left in search of employment, and that it had been necessary to make an organized appeal to the people of the country for help.

At once the little items in the "local and otherwise" columns of the Spring Valley papers showed by dozens how the people began to feel the whip of want.

"Andrew Kerwick started off last week to seek employment elsewhere."

"The Henning Hotel, run by Mrs. John Dixon, was shut up by chattel mortgage foreclosure Friday for $1,200 due the Spring Valley Coal Company for groceries out of the company's store."

" Rumors that 'Mr. So-and-so has closed up' are getting numerous."

" M. L. Leffman has moved his store from this city to Joliet."

" All the freight trains have been taken off the Chicago & North-Western Railroad entering this city but one."

" The mining situation looks very gloomy. At the Joliet meeting the mine-owners showed by their absence that they did not want to discuss the question (with the miners). * * An all summer's idleness is probable."

" Tuesday W. T. Plumb took down his big watch sign, and packed up his stock of watches, jewelry, etc., and shipped them to Tiskilwa, whither he went the same day to open his new store."

" Considerable firewood from over the river [there was coal everywhere beneath them, but they were forbidden to dig it] is being hauled into town."

" Italian miners from this city have been asking for help from people living on the south side of the river." This only two weeks after the shut-down, and there are no thriftier, more faithful workmen than the Italians. They could have saved if any workman could, and the last thing any workman will do is to beg.

" Many Italians have left town for the iron mines of Michigan," two weeks after the lock-out.

" It is estimated that at least two-thirds of the male population have left town to seek work elsewhere." This was four weeks after the lock-out.

" Tuesday, the Miners' National Progressive Union sent wagons out from this city in all directions asking for aid for the miners and their families." This action by the associated miners of the town — only four weeks after the shut-down — shows how poorly paid the whole body had been, how they had been weakened by their winter of self-sacrifice, and how quickly the siege of starvation made itself felt.

During the dreadful months that followed, when thousands of women and children and the men, who could not get work, lived or more correctly, starved on twenty-four cents' worth of flour, meal, etc., a week, the public never had the pleasure of hearing that one dollar or one word of sympathy or regret came from you. Consider such a case as that of Mrs. Mike M——. She has seven children.

Her husband, locked out, went as far away as the coal mines of Missouri for work, but found it at last at Stanton, in this State. During his absence she felt the hour of her confinement approaching. She sent for a doctor. He refused to come. But baby came, although the doctor wouldn't, and, in this hour of supreme trial of womanhood, she was alone—unless God was there. A kindly neighbor came in later and helped her. As she told me this, sitting sick and forlorn in a room in which the furniture and wall paper seemed soaked with misery and malaria, she was shaking with ague. Her baby was a fortnight old, but up to that moment she had had neither medicine nor a doctor. The Chicago, Milwaukee & St. Paul Railroad sent supplies and medicines and physicians to its suffering miners at Braceville, but that is not your kind of political economy.

Not only did the company do nothing to alleviate this misery, part of the tactics of money-making, but, on the contrary, through your spokesman, you threw public ridicule and reproach on those who came forward to mend the lives you had broken. In his public letter to the governor of September 25th, your spokesman characterized the appeals which had been made to the country at large for aid as " falsehood and slander, perhaps without a parallel in the industrial history of the country." In his letter to the Chicago *Times* of October 8th he said, referring to Mayor Cregier's visit to Spring Valley:

" And yet high officials in your city, men who make laws as well as those whose duty it is to execute them, can find time, under the cloak of 'sweet charity,' to sanction the lawless condition referred to when within sight of their office windows, or within one ward of your city, more genuine cases of destitution and misery can be found than could be found in twenty Spring Valleys."

This word " starvation " is obnoxious to you and other gentlemen who cut off the livelihood of working people by light-fingering the " laws" of supply and demand. It grates on your ears. You laugh at it over your weary and heavy-laden dinner tables. You pooh-pooh it when it gets into the newspapers or the appeals for relief. You quiet your conscience, and the generosity of others, by declaring that there is no want, that the people have saved piles of money out of the munificent wages you have paid them, and that they could all go to work to-morrow, and " earn $2 and $3 a day if it were not that they preferred

charity to work." This is a mightily important point with you, and you maintain it with
a stiff upper lip.   Everywhere this sort of talk
scattered by you through parlors, bank directors' rooms, counting-houses, and among your
acquaintances, has tremendous influence.   It
buttresses you and your kind of "business"
men in their determination to believe that the
workingmen can neither do good nor feel
wrongs.   It shuts many hands and pockets
ready to contribute to the relief which partly
defeated your attempts to make the people so
faint with want that their "supply" would
yield to your "demand."   Success in making
the public believe the mystery that your workingmen continue to have plenty to eat after
you have cut off all their means of buying
food is vital to you, and you know it well.
The public endures the things that are being
done all over this country to whole communities of workingmen, only because it does not
understand them.   Even when they are explained, it cannot believe that the strong would
so ill use the weak.   It has not come to see
that our market morality has overgrown all
other morality, and has brought men who
would be good but for business, down to the
depravity of believing that " the Golden Rule "

is that any rule is right which puts gold into their pockets.

There is one fatal flaw in your nervous talk about these poor people preferring, as you say, charity to work.   They worked up to the last minute you kept your mines open.   It was only when you drove them out that they began to beg.   If you had any sense of shame, even any sense of humor, grim as it would be here, you would not make yourselves targets for public indignation and ridicule, by throwing slanders so obviously untrue at the heads of the people who came to Spring Valley to get the " steady work " you advertised, and who worked until you stopped them.

If the world had not learned by the experience of thousands of years how the oppressor hardens his heart at the sight of the suffering he creates, it would be impossible to understand your cynical denial that any distress followed your refusal of all work to the entire community of 5,000 people at Spring Valley. No one but you who are fortified behind hundreds of millions of dollars would dare to deny it.   No one but those who were to make money out of it would want to deny it.   Over against these vain attempts to ignore the palpable truth is the testimony of a cloud of witnesses, reporters of newspapers of all shades of political and economic belief, clergymen, mayors of the surrounding cities, the neighboring farmers, the editors of the local journals, representatives of the State government, and impartial observers who visited Spring Valley to see with their own eyes the extent of the distress in order that they might report upon it to those who wanted to help the stricken people.

"How can you tell when a family is in want?" was asked of the wife of a merchant of Spring Valley, who has done what she could out of the ruin of her husband's business to help those still more unfortunate.

"There's many ways of telling; although some of these poor people would rather die than let their wants be known. When the neighbors see the little children of a family hanging about the door, crying silently hour by hour, they know well enough what's the matter. There's never a bite in that house, you may be sure."

The Chicago *Daily News*, in a telegram from Spring Valley of June 1st, said, a month after the lock out:

The situation of the locked-out miners of Spring Valley has been getting worse every day. What money they had is nearly spent. Friday morning a committee of miners was sent to Chicago to solicit aid. The committee took along a circular to present to the various labor organizations, making a strong appeal for aid for starving families.

The paragraphs given above from the local papers show how simultaneously the work stopped, and the distress began. As early as June 24th, a reporter of the Chicago *Tribune* telegraphed from Spring Valley:

About 500 miners' families are being helped by the relief committee here. Some of the families are dependent entirely on the committee for support, and it is poor support they get, for provisions come in slowly. Aid to the amount of $700 or $800 has been received, which, divided up, would be only about $12.20 in seven weeks to a family, and a family averages six or seven persons. But even this has long ago been mostly given out. One-fourth of the miners in town do not know where their next meal is coming from,

Shortly after the shut-down of the mines a relief committee was organized, who sent sub-committees out in all directions with wagons through the country seeking aid. In this they were quite successful, the farmers contributing liberally day after day and week after week. Besides the committee wagons, private families have scoured the country for anything eatable. A farmer living about seven miles north of town told your correspondent recently that as many as seven and eight parties had been at his farm begging in a single day, and that as high as twenty had been there in a week.

The Boston *Herald*, in its issue of July 27th, had a dispatch announcing that " Mayor Cregier of Chicago, Congressman Frank Lawler, and other members of the relief committee had

left Chicago with several car-loads of provisions
and supplies for the starving locked-out coal
miners of Spring Valley. There are about
2,000 idle miners in the district, making, with
their families, about 6,000 souls. The arrival
of the train there this afternoon was greeted
with great demonstrations of joy. Everywhere there were evidences of the most pinching poverty and destitution. Men, women
and children were most scantily clad in the
cheapest of materials, and there was a great
dearth of foot-gear among them. Their faces
bore unmistakable evidences of pinching hunger. These people have been locked out
nearly three months, and are absolutely on the
verge of starvation."

Besides the tons of provisions, Mayor Cregier brought with him a check for $1,562,
which he presented to Treasurer William Scaife,
of the Miners' District Organization.

" I come," the mayor said, " as the representative of the people of Chicago, who never
hear of want without doing all in their power
to relieve it."

The Spring Valley correspondent of the
Chicago *Tribune* telegraphed, August 6th:
" By dint of close economy the miners manage
to get enough to live on. Many of their fam-

ilies have only flour and a little salt pork from one week's end to another. Many of them do not taste fresh meat from one Sunday to another."

In an interview with a reporter at Springfield, of the Chicago *Tribune*, in July, Secretary Wines said: " At Spring Valley in particular, the apparent destitution greatly impressed me. There are no gardens there, and few cows, pigs, or chickens. The town presents the appearance of a funeral. It is too quiet even for Sunday. The miners there cannot be said to be on a strike in the strict sense of the term. They were ordered out before they had a chance to strike."

The New York *World* of Saturday, August 3d, printed the following special dispatch from Spring Valley:

Her Twin Babes Died of Starvation.

[SPECIAL TO THE WORLD.]

SPRING VALLEY, Ill., Aug. 2.—One of the saddest cases of destitution among the striking miners on record here came to the notice of a *World* correspondent to-day. It was the case of a mother, the wife of one of the locked-out miners, who lost her two babes, twins, for the want of sufficient nourishment to foster them. Being in the poorest circumstances, and living off such charity as was given by the relief committee, she had the misery of seeing her babes die of starvation while holding them to her barren breast.

When the attention of Dr. John H. Rauch,

secretary of the State Board of Health, was called to this, he had only this to say: " That it was a thing frequently found even in more prosperous communities "— a singular product of American prosperity.

In a special article in its issue of August 3d, the New York *World*, under the headlines " Dying to Escape Slavery — that's what the coal. miners of northern Illinois are doing," — said of the whole field:

" There have been scores of deaths among young and old, since the strike; nearly every one of them directly traceable to lack of food, medicine, or medical attendance."

In their report to the governor, Messrs. Gould and Wines say of the state of things up to August: *

" It remains to speak of the suffering caused by the strike. It is real and it is great. There have been no actual cases of starvation. Miners freely divide with each other, and it is warm weather, when vegetables are plenty. But there have been cases in which families have lived for a longer or shorter time on vegetables alone. There has been suffering, also, in sickness, for want of medicines and proper medi-

* Report of the Coal-Miners' Strike and Lock-Out in Northern Illinois, by J. M. Gould and Fred. H. Wines, special commissioners appointed by the governor, August, 1889, pages 22-23.

cal attendance. It needs no official investigation to prove that ten thousand men, who have been idle for nearly four months, and who had not much money or supplies laid away, but who have families to support, must be by this time in a condition verging on destitution. They do not parade their suffering; they conceal it rather, especially from their employers, knowing that the operators rely upon this suffering to bring them sooner or later to terms. The miners in this district, as we have shown, were receiving about $225,000 a month in wages, which would (after deducting one-eighth) amount, by the 1st of September, to nearly $800,000, which they have lost; they are that much on the wrong side of the ledger. What they had, they have been consuming; they have been exhausting their credit; many of them have mortgaged their homes. Whether they have done right or wrong, this state of affairs cannot last long. The supplies which have been sent them, generous as they have been, have been ridiculously inadequate in proportion to the number of mouths to be fed. These men do not want charity; what they want is work and wages. If $7,500 a day in wages was inadequate for their comfort, and they quit work because it was proposed to give them

5

less, will less than $7,500 a day in charity be
sufficient to supply their needs?   And is there,
can there be, any hope of help to this amount,
for any length of time? The real necessity for
aid from outside has been acknowledged, at
least by the Chicago, Milwaukee & St. Paul
Railway, which has hired a physician for its
miners at Braceville, and sent a supply of
necessaries for sick women and children, to be
given out by its agent, in accordance with the
doctor's recommendation."

On August 11th a car-load of provisions was
sent to Spring Valley from Peoria.   The New
York *World* described the occurrence under
the heading : " In Starvation's Grim Grip."   It
said :

" One thousand men and women in a starving condition tramped down from Spring
Valley to the Rock Island depot at midnight,
and waited hours for a car-load of provisions
which was on the way, accompanied by Mayor
Warner of Peoria, and members of the relief
committee of that city.   The crowd went wild
with delight when they heard of this relief, and
paraded the streets with torches.   The mayor
brought with him $400 in cash, and said that
Peoria would send ten more car-loads, if necessary.   Everybody, he said, had contributed,

even to the women who sell vegetables in the city market. Part of the provisions were distributed at once. This makes the third carload of provisions that has reached Spring Valley in thirty days." Three car-loads in a month for five hundred families !

In the news items circulated by the associated press was this one dated at Galesburg, Ill., August 22d:

Five Spring Valley women, with infants in their arms, came here to beg provisions and clothing for the families of miners there. The mayor sent them to a boarding house. They will not be suffered to beg, but a committee of citizens will canvass the place for them. They represent the families of Spring Valley strikers as in a very destitute condition, and say that the women have gone out in companies to the leading cities of the State to beg for their children.

The following paragraph which appeared in the *Sentinel*, a weekly paper of Spring Valley, August 31st, used stronger language about the " misery" there than any of the preceding, and the writer lived a daily witness of what he described:

The fact that the wives and children of miners are dying of starvation, right in the garden of the world and the center of the " land of the brave and home of the free," is not a very consoling spectacle for a Christian country to present to the world. Then, when such suffering, destitution and death, are the result of an attempt of coal operators, protected by a tariff of 75 cents a ton on coal, to starve laborers into submission to a reduction of wages, the sight is one that should forever damn the system and the soulless capitalist that it protects.

The New York *World* sent a representative through the northern Illinois coal-mining district, and in his letter of August 25th, he describes what he saw at Spring Valley. Among other things he says:

" As we passed the little cemetery, with a plain stone here and there marking the resting-places of those who had lived in better times, I noticed that there were many freshly dug graves, little mounds that told of recent burials, and empty graves yawning for an occupant. These evidences of the lock-out's fearful work told a tale which could not be expressed in words. They told of want of food, medicine, medical care and nourishment!   *   *   *
The site of the company houses at Spring Valley is as inimical to the health of the occupants as at Clarke and Coal Cities. The corporation has selected, because of its cheapness, the elevation which overhangs the Illinois River, on which to erect the miners' houses. The air of this spot is impregnated with malaria, from which the residents are almost continually suffering. The death-rate of this town is large, even when the mines are in operation, and the sick-list is equal to that of a healthier

town five times its size. From a cursory ex-
amination, it is a low estimate to say that seven
out of every ten families are sick—seriously so.
Malarial fevers, diphtheria, cholera morbus,
ague and pneumonia form the bulk of the ail-
ments. When lack of medical care and medicine is added to the unavoidable sickness, is
it any wonder that scores of men, women and
children have found a last resting-place in the
cemetery since the lock-out?   *   *   *
There are 1,200 heads of families in Spring
Valley who have not had a stroke of work
since last May, and half of these families have
had nothing to eat except what the charitable
have given them. Salt pork, potatoes and
corn-meal, with a little tea and coffee, have
been their sole means of subsistence throughout the lock-out. Such food is unfit for sick
and delicate women and children to eat, and
the coffin is soon seen to leave the house.
*   *   *   Yet these poor people did
not denounce their oppressors; did not heap
maledictions on the heads of those responsible
for their condition.   *   *   *
" The policy of the Spring Valley Company
has been to always keep a surplus of miners
on hand, and employ more men than were
actually needed, so that the company would

sell more goods at its 'truck' store, rent more of its houses, keep the men so poor that they would be unable to resist the reduction in wages, and create discord in the ranks when a strike occurred. A grave moral responsibility rests on the heads of the mine-owners, who have inveigled married men to this barren spot and now cast them off to starve with their wives and children.   *   *   *

  " After dinner I took a walk with members of the relief committee through the desolate place. The family of Sylvester McDonnell numbers fourteen, from grandparents to grand-children, and they occupied two three-roomed houses. They were drawn up in battle array outside their home as I approached to talk with their grandfather. They were in rags and tatters, pinched faces and hollow cheeks showing that the cupboard had often been empty. 'I fought for the negroes,' exclaimed the old man, ' and now I am fighting for my-self and the folks. It's the principle of the thing I am starving for. I am an American citizen, and I claim the right to educate my children as Americans should be educated. We offered to go to work here for a year with-out a cent if the company would only keep us in clothing and food, send our children to school, and pay our rent if we didn't live in one of their houses. They wouldn't do it, and that shows we cannot live on the reduced wages without begging or going into debt.' "

At about the same time, Father Huntington, of New York, of the order of the Holy Cross, who devotes his life to work among the poor, visited the mining regions on an errand of mercy. He was greatly moved by what he saw, and gave it eloquent and indignant utterance. In an interview in the Chicago *News*, he said:

" It is bad enough everywhere I went, but it is worse at Spring Valley than elsewhere. But even there the poverty-stricken inhabitants are not like the poor I am used to seeing in New York. There is no whining; the people show intelligence and pride; even hunger has not debased their feelings, as one might expect. I am used to scenes of want, but what I saw at Spring Valley was different. It was more pitiful than anything I ever witnessed before. I went among the cottages. They are nice, and are surrounded by pretty lawns and gardens, but the awful poverty within was shocking.   *   *   *   Sickness is increasing, and the doctors told me the people were so enfeebled by long privation and

anxiety, that an epidemic might break out at any moment. Business is utterly dead. *
* * What is the outlook? Well, it is black enough. The mine-owners profit whether the mines are operated or not."

To a reporter in New York, Father Huntington said:

" I visited Spring Valley. In that town there is already cruel destitution, and, unless aid is sent them very soon, many will die of want and the diseases induced by insufficient nourishment. Even now there is an epidemic of diphtheria among the children, and much ague among the adults, which a few cents' worth of quinine would have prevented, but which could not be obtained. There are between five and six thousand persons in the town, and 2,360 are on the relief list. The Company has ordered the mines to be shut down for an indefinite period, and the town will be wiped out as effectually as was Johnstown by the Conemaugh flood. If the people of this country desire to avert what will be a national calamity, they should help those miners of Spring Valley at once. * * * My patriotism, too, was outraged when I found that men who had come from England, a so-called effete monarchy, were compelled to labor under conditions abolished in the country of their birth twenty years before. I found in existence the contract and the "truck" or store-order system, together with monthly payments."

September 9th the Rev. John F. Power, the Catholic priest of Spring Valley, wrote the following letter in answer to an inquiry from a friend in Chicago:

SPRING VALLEY, ILL., September 9.

DEAR SIR.—In reply to yours of the 7th, asking a statement from me as to the condition of my people, I desire to say that fully one-half of them are still dependent on outside charity for the necessaries of life. Most of the men are away looking for work. Some succeed at once, but it takes at least a month to realize any cash to send home to wife and little ones. Meanwhile their families are in a precarious condition, even when sickness spares them. I am going to appeal in person, in such parishes as I can obtain permission, to the charitable for aid for my congregation, beginning next Sunday in the cathedral parish, Peoria. I have upward of 300 pupils in the sisters' school. Besides maintaining the school, we must do what we can to clothe the children coming on cold weather. This is why I go abroad begging as the only alternative to closing the school and sending away the sisters.   JOHN F. POWER.

From then until the end of the lock-out Father Power spent every Sunday in " going abroad begging " in more prosperous parishes, for the funds with which to keep the children alive and the schools open.

The writer of this story went to Spring Valley September 3d, to learn at first hand the

facts of the destitution, and, as the result of
his observations, published an appeal for help
through the Chicago newspapers and the
Associated Press.   In it he said:

"There is greater need than ever of help for
the starving men, women and children of
Spring Valley, in this State.

"There are thousands suffering there from
want of food, clothing, medicine and sympathy.

"Most of these sufferers are children, and
most of the children are little ones.

"I have just returned from Spring Valley.
There, in this great and prosperous State, and
in the midst of harvest-laden farms and rich
cities, the visitor will see a cemetery of the
living.   Instead of the light of health, there
shines in the eyes of the men and women the
phosphorescence of decaying strength, and
the children, fatally weakened by want, are
dying.

"There are families where adults and children, grievously sick, are without medical attendance or medicines, because there is no
money to pay for them."

September 29th, after a second visit, the
writer published a second appeal for relief, in
which he said:

Among other means of getting intelligent and unbiased information as to the exact state of things I visited the Catholic
school and the public school, in which together there are over
600 children, and talked with the teachers and many of the
children.   The sisters who teach in the Catholic school said
that their children gave unmistakable evidence of not having
sufficient food.   They were paler than the year before, and they
could not study as well.   Children would frequently fall asleep
at their desks from weakness.   But so sturdy was their pride
and self-respect that it was almost impossible for their teacher
to obtain from them any acknowledgment that they did not get
enough to eat at home.   Children who were unmistakably suffering for want of nourishment would even refuse food when
offered them by their teacher, and in some cases the sister
superior said when food was taken by some such child, it was
immediately rejected by the stomach, showing how far the ex-
haustion of hunger had gone.   One of the teachers in the public school stated that on her way to the school in the morning
she would sometimes meet as many as a dozen of her class out
with baskets going to beg.   As they saw her the little things,
ashamed, would try to hide from sight until she had passed.
In both schools numbers of the children were insufficiently
clothed, little boys and girls of the tenderest years having on
only some light sack or jacket, with no underclothing.   It was
a cold, bleak day, but many were barefoot.   How the people
have lived at all is a mystery.   There have been during the last
four weeks ending September 25th five distributions by the relief
committee — all in goods, no money has been given out — and
the extent of this "charity" is sufficiently indicated by the
statement taken from the account of the committee that each
family of seven, and others in proportion, had received for the
entire period of four weeks flour, meat, etc., to the value of
$5.88, or 84 cents' worth for each person for the whole four
weeks.   The mayor of the city, the editor of the Spring Valley
Gazette, the Congregational clergyman, Mr. Stringer, all the
physicians of the place, every one in fact stated without qualifi-
cation that were it not for the relief from without the people

would have starved and would be starving. To live on such an allowance is to live a life of slow death by starvation, and the faces of the people, especially the little women and little men, show it. The death rate shows it, and with the first touch of cold and wet weather will show it in terrible shape unless kindlier hearts come to the rescue.

The undertaker, Mr. Dyer, who has had the largest number of interments, had kept no account of them, but, speaking from memory, said that during the last three months he had averaged five a week, most of them children, and most of these cases of diphtheria. Dr. Coveney has had thirty-five cases of this disease in the last six weeks. The local press, I was told, reported seven deaths from diphtheria last week. There is a great deal of malarial sickness among young and old.

Notwithstanding all the denials, official and other, it is true that these poor people, women and children, have been refused medicine and medical attendance.

I went to see Mrs. Dennis M——. She was in bed shivering with a chill. In her arms was a little child a few weeks old, who had been ill for several days with inflammation of the lungs or throat, she thought, but did not know. She had sent for Dr. ——. He had refused to come. She then obtained an order from the town supervisor to Dr. —— to go at the expense of the county, as provided by law. The doctor refused to go. The town supervisor then called upon him in person. The doctor refused to go. I went to see the doctor, and stated the deplorable situation of the mother and child to him. He admitted the facts of the official order to him, and his refusal, and added: "I haven't gone, and I won't go." And he didn't go*. I gave the woman some of the money sent me by

---

* This statement having been challenged by the doctor referred to, whose name will — with more mercy than he has shown the sick poor — be omitted here, there was published in the Chicago *Tribune* the following sworn statement by the town supervisor, Mr. O'Hara, showing that orders given by him in person and in writing have been disregarded, and the sick left unattended:

" State of Illinois, {
" Bureau County. }

" James O'Hara, being duly sworn, deposes and says that he called on Dr. —— in person, and requested him to visit Mrs. M——n, who had

Miss ——, and, when I visited Mrs. M—— the next day, she had had a doctor and some medicine, and knew for the first time what was the matter with her baby, which if it recovers owes its life to the dear lady in New York.   The father and husband here was locked out last spring, and went away from home to seek work, and has recently succeeded in finding employment at Clark City.

I visited Mrs. Louis J——.   Her husband, locked out like all the other miners, went away for employment, and is laid up at Sparling sick with ague, having been able to do but three days' work since spring.   Of her four children three are ill with chills and fever, one of these a baby in the cradle.   The last had croup the night before.   She had sent for Dr. ——.   He had refused to come, and up to the time I saw her she had had neither medicine nor medical attendance.

"Why don't the men go to work instead of living on charity?"   There were once 2,500 miners there.   As Adjutant-General Vance states, there are now but 250 left.   The rest have gone.   They have scattered themselves to the four quarters for work.   They have gone as far away as Wyoming, Kentucky, Tennessee, Iowa and Missouri.   A short time ago an agent of the Union Pacific mines, at Rock Springs, came to Spring Valley.   He wanted forty men.   Ninety presented themselves.   He took his pick, and left fifty men to seek another disappointment.   The men are leaving every day, as they get opportunity.   They often arrive at their destination to find that they have been deceived.   They write back, the postmistress is told by their wives, that they can sometimes barely make their board.

---

called at his house for an order for medical assistance, and that Dr. —— refused to do so; that the next morning he called on Dr. —— again, and asked him to visit an aged couple, and again mentioned the case of Mrs. M——n, and that Dr. —— still refused to visit her; that on September 29th a Mrs. M—l—n called on him for an order to Dr. —— for medical attendance; that he gave her the order, and it was ignored by Dr. ——, he refusing to render her family medical attention.

"JAMES O'HARA,
"Supervisor of Hall Town.
"Subscribed and sworn to before me this second day of October, 1889.
"J. R. DAVIDSON,
"Police Magistrate for the City of Spring Valley, County and State aforesaid."

A miner thus changing his place of work frequently has to buy new tools, costing from $15 to $25. Still, the records of the postoffice, which I saw, show that the men who are hunting abroad for the means of life for the wives and children they have left behind, to face, unprotected, the dangers of famine and disease, are sending home from $125 to $200 a week in all.

County Agent Foley, of Chicago, who had done a great deal to collect and forward relief, received the following letter which continues the deplorable record into the month of October, and throws light on the difficulties which the men experienced in finding work elsewhere:

SPRING VALLEY, ILL., Oct. 4.

Mr. John Foley, Chicago.

DEAR SIR: Yours of the 3d inst. at hand. The car-load of provisions sent by you the 2d has been received, and is being distributed to-day.

Many of our men have gone in various directions in search of work. Some who have gone in answer to the many advertisements sent here for miners and others who have gone with agents find that those places are not as represented, the conditions being such that they could scarcely make their board, consequently they would not be able to send their families any assistance. There are now 476 families being supplied by the relief committee. There are a great many cases of sickness, mainly malaria and ague, and a few cases of diphtheria. The medicine sent by Mr. Lloyd has done much to relieve this, as heretofore it was a hard matter to procure medicines. The coming cold weather will greatly add to the needs of all.

A. D. BOURKE, President.
THOMAS BRADY,
Secretary of the Miners' Union.

The Hon. Frank Lawler, one of the members of Congress from Chicago, nobly gave nearly his whole summer to investigating the sufferings and wrongs of the miners of Spring Valley, Braidwood, and other places in Illinois, and eloquently and fearlessly appealed for relief and for justice through the press, public meetings and by personal solicitation. If this was done " for political effect " so much the better. It is high time the servants of the people sought to win their favor by serving them against the ruthless plutocracy which is oppressing them.

" Thanks to the human heart by which we live, thanks to its tenderness," the public responded to the appeals for help with enough food, clothing, medicine, and sympathy to take off the sharpest edge of the distress, though it did not give enough to save the miners at last from a disastrous and humiliating defeat.

Why did not this evidence, volumes of which have been laid before you by the daily press of all parties and opinions, melt your hearts? Has the bourbonism of the " divine right " of buying cheap and selling dear become so fanatical that you think you have a right to grind up the very bodies of the poor for " six per

cent. on the capital"—watered capital at that?
Have your riches and your use of agents
to deal with your employés and customers,
borne you so far away from the people
that you do really not believe that they
have hearts that can ache as yours can, bodies
that can suffer as yours can? Don't you believe that they love their wives and children
as you do yours? that their hearts sink as
yours would, when, without warning, they are
dispersed, penniless, into strange parts for
work, leaving wives and babies behind, perhaps to starve? Don't you believe that want
of food weakens their bodies as it would
yours — that hope and success and sympathy
are as essential to their well-being as to your
" finer " natures?

If you don't like to lose one per cent. out
of your six per cents., how do you think it
makes poor men feel to have you cut off all
their income? If you like to take your wives
and children with you to the sea-shore or to
Europe, how do you think a workman feels
when you force him to tramp hundreds of
miles away from his family, leaving them to
charity, while he hunts for work, as if that,
too, were charity? Is it having three good

meals a day that has made you believe that to live on twenty-one cents worth of pork and meal a week is not " starvation " ?

CHAPTER VII.

BUYING BRETHREN BELOW COST.

THE local press chronicled your lock-out in a curt six-line paragraph, closing with the statement that " the wages for the next year is the question now to be decided." That was the question, but it was not to be decided by the ordinary and decent processes of bargaining between two free parties. It was to be decided by a commercial attack of the strong upon the very lives of the weak. These were to be made helpless, then asked to make a *free* contract. You who could live in luxury indefinitely without giving employment took employment away from the workman, who must die without it. You took hope, too, away. When you were boomers, you fed the people on hope in lieu of the good wages you had promised; but, when you changed this rôle and began to play the Doomer, it was necessary for success in bringing down the people that despair should be added to disease and starvation. Dark hints were circulated from

(82)

headquarters as to what the millionaires had done in other cases and would do in this.   The leader in this war on the workingmen, it was said, had utterly destroyed one mining town which had resisted his will, and he would do so here to obtain what he wanted.   Meanwhile what he wanted remained like the secret of the sphinx — uncommunicated.   " The Coal Company," said the Spring Valley *Gazette* of May 8th, " are as yet non-committal, and have made no offer to the men."   At a mass-meeting of the miners June 1st, the resolutions began with this preamble, which corroborates the above: " WHEREAS, The Spring Valley Coal Company, have locked us out since April 29th without having given us any information why they did so."   The coal company's office gazed out upon the town, blankly through its two great plate-glass eyes, and made no sign. The workingmen wrote letters to the company asking when and how they could get work, but could obtain no answer.   They offered arbitration, but in vain.   They sent committees to the office, but were told that positive instructions had been given that the men should be dealt with only as individuals, never again through representatives.

During all this time the only communication

vouchsafed them was the serving of eviction notices in July on all the families that were living in the company's houses.

Though the eviction notices were served with all the due legal formalities required, the eviction did not follow. It is an open secret that the then superintendent broke out into open rebellion against the ruthlessness with which the company was carrying out its policy.

Not long after he sold his stock, and left the service of the company. Another reason for the arrest of the policy of evictions was that it was plain that public opinion was too much roused to submit to it. The case of Spring Valley had become a *cause celebre*. Things that had been done and could have been done in the dark, it was not safe to do in the blaze of publicity which now poured in there.

This news item from Spring Valley of July 22d, illustrates the methods used to terrorize the workingman into submitting to the company's demands. It is a vivid picture of the influence brought to bear upon the men, as a preliminary to asking them to sign " free contracts," and throws a flood of sunshine on the kindly means used by " capital" to demonstrate its " harmony of interest " with labor.

WILL EVICT IDLE MINERS.

Notices Already Served by the Sheriff—Probabilities of Resistance by the Men.

SPRING VALLEY, ILL., July 22.—To-night nearly 100 notices to vacate have been served by the Spring Valley Coal Company upon the idle miners, and about twenty-five more will be served to-morrow. One week from to-day eviction notices proper will be served. Two weeks from to-day Sheriff Henderson and an armed posse of deputies will enforce the notices and turn all idle miners out. There will doubtless be a total of about 650 persons thrown out. The coal company says that the law will be enforced to the letter, while the miners will resist—some by force some by legal means. Where the miners will go is a mystery. But few have any money to pay their way to other towns, and there are not enough empty houses in town to keep them. The houses will be boarded up as fast as emptied.

From April 29th until August 23d your contemptuous silence in the face of all inquiries as to the cause and prospects of the lock-out was maintained — five heart-sick months for the people of Spring Valley. Then the company posted in its windows at Spring Valley an offer to them of thirty-five cents a ton, instead of ninety cents, which they were receiving when the mines were closed. The following is the notice which was posted at the Spring Valley mines, on Thursday, August 22, 1889:

NOTICE TO MINERS.—I am directed by the president of this company to make the miners of Spring Valley the following proposition, viz.: Seventy-five cents per ton for mining in the third vein, with thirty inches of brushing and three men in a room, from now until May 1, 1890. I am also directed that

men now occupying company houses, who are unwilling to work
on these terms, or who do not begin to work on or before Monday, September 2, prox., must vacate the houses occupied by
them on or before that date, or we will be obliged to proceed to
regain possession peaceably and lawfully.   The president of this
company desires it to be further understood that we shall not
treat with any committee representing any organization in the
future, and that each man will have to seek employment for
himself and individually.

(Signed)   THE GENERAL MANAGER.

This offer was so worded that, to the unin-
itiated, it might seem an offer of seventy-five
cents a ton.   The words " seventy-five cents
a ton " occurred in it, but there was a string
tied to them, in the shape of conditions, which
cost the miners forty cents a ton.   The offer
was, in substance, " seventy-five cents a ton,
less forty cents worth of your work and time."
No one understood the true character of the
offer better than the men who would have had
to work under it, and no one has explained
it better than they did in a communication
which they immediately addressed to the public.

" Brushing," so often referred to below, is
the work of removing the rock above the
coal, so as to give head-room for the mules
and pit-cars.   The company require that the
roadway be nine feet wide at the bottom, eight
feet wide at the top and about six feet high.
Of this space, from three feet to three and one-

half feet in height is coal, for removing which
the miners are paid the agreed rate per ton,
whatever that may be.   Underneath the coal is
a layer of fire-clay, sometimes of very hard
sandstone, which the miner has to dig away,
without pay, and above the coal is solid rock,
which he has to dig away for head-room, without pay, to the height of twenty-four inches
above the coal, and for a width of eight feet.
The company used to pay the miners for this
" brushing" at the rate of $1.25 a yard, but
it has gradually shifted the burden of it on the
miners of doing it gratuitously.   Before the
lock-out the company had put sixteen inches
of this unpaid work on them, and it has now
increased this to twenty-four inches.   A considerable part, also, of the work on the coal
vein itself is without compensation.   The men
get no pay for the nut coal, which drops
through the spaces of the coal-screens, about
one-eighth of all mined.   And there is in the
Spring Valley coal a seam of sulphur, one to
two inches wide, and a band of iron pyrites
varying from one to several inches in thickness.
The coal that breaks into " nut," the sulphur
and the pyrites yield the miners nothing but
unrequited toil.   There are many other time-
consuming labors connected with coal-mining

which cannot easily be described to the unin-
itiated, but all may be summed up in the statement that, of the ten hours spent hard at work
on the knees, or lying down hundreds of feet
below daylight, only about two-thirds produce
actual earnings to the miner.

This is the letter to the public explaining the
" offer " of 35 cents a ton :

SPRING VALLEY, Ill., Aug. 24.

Editor of the Herald:

We wish, through the columns of the *Herald* to give the people of Chicago and elsewhere a proper idea of the proposition
of the company which was made to the miners here yesterday
morning; viz., 75 cents per ton, thirty inches of brushing and
three men in a place.   Also that the men must treat individually with the company, they refusing to recognize committees or any " board " acting for the men as a whole, which
practically means that all persons who have been active in their
endeavors to have some degree of justice done them will not get
any work here or anywhere else if they can hinder them.

Now, 75 cents per ton is a reduction of 15 cents, the previous price being 90 cents in the Spring Valley and La Salle district.   Thirty inches of brushing means at least 10 cents per
ton more, as we were previous to the lock-out paid $1.25 per
yard for this amount of brushing.

It has been stated in the press by some one writing from here
(who is unknown to us) that previous to the lock-out the men
were working three in a place, which is not the fact.   We simply
divided our work with those that had been thrown out of work
by the closing down last December of mines 2 and 4.   At no
time were we working three in a place together, but were
working two men, each man laying off two days in the week.
As will readily be seen, this was to each man a reduction of two
days in the week, or one-third of his time, and this was not understood to be permanent, but only until mines Nos. 2 and 4

would resume operations, as the mines, when running at their fullest capacity, would not, and did not, give the men full work with two in a place. The forcing of three men in a place would simply be dividing the work and wages of two men between three. Now, to sum up the proposition : In the first place, there is proposed a reduction of 15 cents per ton, from 90 to 75 cents ; in the next place we are asked to take thirty inches of brushing, for which we were previously paid $1.25 per yard, which is equivalent to 10 cents per ton ; and last, but not least, three men in a place, which, as we have shown, means a reduction of one-third of the earnings of each man, which is one-third of 90, or 30 cents per ton, making in all 55 cents per ton of a reduction. Now, this is a reduction of over one-half our former wages, which were shown by the recent investigation before the State board of charities to be an average of $28 to $30 per month.

By way of properly seasoning this kind and considerate offer, it is further stated in the proposition, that, if the men do not accept these terms on or before the 2d of September, the company will proceed to regain possession of their houses, which, of course, means eviction, as none of the miners have the means to move elsewhere.

This infamous proposition has caused general indignation here, not only among the miners, but also among the business men, who are denouncing the outrage in terms more forcible than polite. The general manager has resigned the management of the mines, and has also sold out his interest in the company. His reason for doing so, it is said, is because of the president's insisting on these terms, which the latter knows can never be agreed to by the men, and also because of his intention of importing colored men to take the place of miners.

A. D. BOURKE, President of Lodge No. 26.
THOMAS BRADY, Secretary of Lodge No. 26.
ROBERT WILSON, Secretary of Relief Committee.

A few days before this " offer," the president of the company had, by an ostentatious withdrawal, broken up a conference between mine-owners and miners struggling for an agreement in Chicago, at the Grand Pacific Hotel.   As he did so, he is reported by one of the newspapers to have said :

" I will settle with my own men.   I do not care what this conference may decide upon. I will pay my men as high a figure as they may fix.   Yes, I will pay them a higher scale than any which may be adopted at this confer- ence, that is, if I continue to mine coal in Illinois.   If I decide to resume the mining of coal, it will be on a bigger scale than ever before, and on an entirely different basis."

This was August 16th.   The value of the promise to pay " as high " as others, or " higher," was illustrated within a week, by the " offer" of August 23d, just described.   This has the unique distinction of being without exception the lowest bid yet made for Ameri- can labor.   According to the estimate of their previous average earnings, made by the special commissioners of the State, it would have yielded the miners about $10 a month — and " find " themselves.   According to your own " statistics," it would have given them about $16 a month, and find themselves.   This offer was stuck to, and repeated publicly a month

later, as the best you could do.   Every one
knows well, that it was never supposed, even in
offering such terms, that they would be listened
to by the men.   Public opinion will never
quarrel with your men for publicly branding as
" infamous" such a proposition, made after
the silence and lock-out of five months, with
every appearance of a purpose to add a new
terror to the apprehensions of the community,
in order to frighten them into selling you their
labor below the cost of subsistence.   No one
but those who made this offer have ever had
the hardihood to defend it.   Even the local
journals of Spring Valley denounced it.   The
Gazette of September 12th, said : " The men
here are willing to do what the La Salle men
are, but the company wants them to accept
terms way below that.   This the miners declare
they will not accept, and the sympathies of our
citizens are with them.   The Spring Valley
Coal Company can certainly pay as high
wages as its competitors."

Stung into protest by this offer to the men,
and the threat to close the mines, the Spring
Valley *Sentinel*, which, with the *Gazette*, con-
stitute the local press of the town, had a plain-
spoken article in its issue of August 31st.   It is
of importance as showing, as the article in the

Gazette does, that the injustice done the miners
was so obvious that it had to be admitted by
local elements not specially friendly to them.
Speaking broadly, the business men and the
working men of our civilization are antag-
onistic to each other, and this is true in little
Spring Valley as in better known communities.
The business men and the working men represent different social classes, and different sides
of the bargains of industry. Their different
circumstances have given them different ideals
and philosophies of life. The business man aims
to make a fortune for himself, and, to reach that
solitary good, wants to go it alone. He must
have " competition," " individual enterprise,"
laissez faire, etc. The working man knows
that solitary prosperity and the good of the
people are compatible only by being made one.
He is forced to seek the good of all as the preliminary of good for himself, and he advocates
the policy of union, self-sacrifice of the individual for the sake of all, social control. Personal inquiry among the merchants of Spring
Valley showed that in most cases they felt the
prejudices of their class against the workingmen and their ideas, although this prejudice
was often tempered by the kindest personal feelings, and the tenderest commiseration for their

sufferings.   The newspapers of Spring Valley
are supported by the advertisements and sub-
scriptions of the business class, including the
patronage of the coal company itself.   That
these papers spoke out as they did, must be
counted the strongest possible evidence of the
oppressive unfairness of the action of the mine-
owners.

The article in the *Sentinel* was as follows:

THE SITUATION.

The present situation is anything but encouraging for Spring
Valley.   The mines are closed down, and all the clerical force
laid off indefinitely.   The general manager, who owns $350,000,
or one-seventh of the capital stock, offered to take the mines
and run them, and give the company fifteen cents a ton clear
of expenses.*   This was refused by the president of the company.   At Braidwood a settlement is about to be made at 87½
cents per ton.   There is an offer of 82½ cents at La Salle, but
there is little hopes of a settlement here.   The *Sentinel* would
be untrue to its convictions of duty did it not call attention
to the true condition of both sides of this momentous question.
It has been given out that this was the largest coal mining plant
in the United States, truthfully.   The Town Site Company
have advertised and sold a large amount of real estate on these
representations.   The coal company and the Town Site Company are practically indentical.   Men came here and invested
all they possessed, knowing the facts, and believing in the asser-

---

* The president of the Spring Valley Coal Company, in a conference
with the miners about their wages, told them that they could take the
mines and run them, if they would pay him a royalty of only fifteen cents
a ton.   This, to "prove" to the men that the company could not afford to
pay them living wages.   But, when the superintendent, who was also
part owner, did what the poor miners had not the money, or nerve, or
knowledge to do — accepted the proposition, the president backed down
at once.

tions that the coal company would be a lasting feature of the town. The business done here is transacted solely on the money disbursed by the coal company. Men who are engaged in business realize that to stop the mines, stops business. They have waited for four months, and with the announcement that another six months of idleness was in store for them, they have become justly indignant; and are only waiting for a suitable opportunity to unload and seek other and more stable fields of trade. That is one side of the situation. Let us see if there are any extenuating circumstances. The gigantic coal company has lost money here. They cannot pay last year's prices and not lose more. The president of the company makes a proposition which he claims is all he can do. He cannot get men to accept it. After waiting a week, he says: " It is not likely that operations will be resumed for six months or a year." The people of all classes are shocked, and many are panic-stricken. What shall we do? What does it mean? We will tell you. For the business men of the town, six months or a year more of idleness means bankruptcy ; for the workingmen who have depended on this industry for a livelihood, a removal, living on charity or starvation. For the coal company it means a greater loss than has hitherto been sustained; the opening of new mines, if work is ever resumed. And it means a new population when the city is once more brought to life. Now let the candid, intelligent reader judge where justice and self-interest conflict, and then prognosticate the future. The *Sentinel* has this to say:

> Though the mills of God grind slowly,
>   Yet they grind exceeding small ;
> Though with patience he stands waiting,
>   With exactness grinds He all.

And believing in the truth of this, we say there is yet a future for our city, and a prosperous tide of affairs yet to come. The president may legally close his mines now, but if the governor of this State and legislature do their duty as law-makers and executives should, this state of affairs will be regulated, and the rights of innocent parties protected. That there is something radically wrong in the management of this affair we are satisfied. The Union Coal Company, of La Salle, operating the same vein of coal, and presumably has the same market, has a standing offer of 82½ cents. Braidwood operators have made an offer ten cents in advance of our company's proposition. Its president, in his letter to Congressman Lawler, recently published in the Chicago *Tribune*, takes the Chicago market as a basis and says " if the good people of Chicago " will pay such a price for coal, he will open the mines. Now, Chicago is not the Spring Valley Company's market, and never was ; all last year he sold coal to the North-Western road here at this point, Spring Valley, for $1.42 per ton. Here is his market, and all along the line of the North-Western road. Streator is a competitor for a very small part of the coal trade at junction points only. These facts, placed beside the refusal to lease the mines on a fifteen cent royalty, are not consistent with his proposition. The situation is bad. The coal company has made a bad matter very much worse.

The *Gazette* and the *Sentinel* expressed the almost universal opinion condemning the offer of the coal company to its men, and approving their manliness in resenting it as an insult added to injury. The Rev. Mr. Stringer said, in his pulpit Sunday evening, October 27th: "When the president of the company offered the men seventy five cents per ton with thirty inches of brushing and three men in a room, nobody thought the men ought to accept it." All of this is evidence from sources which throughout have been far more partial to the employers than to the men.

Adjutant-General Vance said, after visiting

Spring Valley officially for the governor:
" There is a universal expression [among the
citizens of Spring Valley], that the offer of
seventy-five cents a ton for mining and thirty
inches of brushing, with three men in a room,
would be unreasonable, and an unfair remuneration to the miners, and the president is
charged with insincerity in making the offer."

With this offer of thirty-five cents a ton,
ostensibly seventy-five cents a ton, was coupled
the requirement that the men should abandon
their union. You do all your business through
a union, and by walking, or more correctly
sitting delegates, and through committees
of directors, and you keep a large staff of
"professional agitators" constantly busy on
your behalf in courts and legislatures and
stock exchanges. But because you are rich
and think you have the power, you determined
to take away the same rights from these poor
men. By this demand of August 23d, for the
surrender of their union, the men learned that,
worse than a reduction of wages, the destruction of their union had been decreed. This
meant the destruction of their power to make
a free contract, and to protect themselves
against violations of the contract when made.
It meant that the tasks, hours of work, the

pay, the personal liberty, the treatment at the hands of overseers, settlement of disputes, and other matters, which lay at the very foundations of livelihood and rights, were to depend on the will of the employer — harder than that, on the will of the overseer. It meant that the men were to be denied the benefit of any gift of leadership — always too rare — that might develop itself among them. It meant that any man so gifted, who should have the heart to speak against the abuse of his fellows, who should have the brain to see how they could make better bargains for themselves, and the tongue to get the idea into their heads, and to speak for them, should be banished at the will of the employer. It meant that the workmen could have work only at the price of dumb submission and disunited helplessness.

The employers, rich, remote, independent, could bring their combined power operated through an agent, to bear resistlessly on the men, poor, dependent, anchored to the spot by family responsibilities and lack of the means to get away. The employers, although strong enough to stand alone, were united together in a union the wealth and discipline of which were far beyond anything possible to the

7

workingmen, and yet announced that they were going to take away the same right of union from their men.

The company's vein of coal is so thin that the men have to work all day on their knees or lying down, but you insist that in addition to this they shall come on their knees when they make their application for work, and not like American citizens acting through a committee or attorney, if that suits them better than coming one by one. You have in the mines a class of useful and docile animals in the mules which stay in the depths for years, and sometimes never come back to the surface. You always treat with them "individually." If your plans succeed, it will not be long before you will have the power to keep your miners like your mules — down below from year's end to year's end. There will be nothing left them worth coming to the surface for, because, if you can make them give up their unions, you can make them give up everything. " Unite or Die " said Franklin to the American colonies. The unorganized workman, says Prof. Thorold Rogers, cannot make a free contract. John Morley, the great English statesman, said recently to the miners of Durham : " We all know what the labor union has done for the

working people.   It has made men of them."
You, with so many millions you could not
count them if you counted all your life like
clerks of the treasury, instead of helping to
make men of your workingmen, seek to dehu-
manize them for " more " millions.

The indignant refusal of the miners to consider the offer of August 23d as anything
but a brutality was followed by the closing of
the company's offices in Spring Valley.   A
special dispatch in the Chicago *Herald* of
August 26th, said:

SPRING VALLEY, Ill., August 26.—A telegram was received
here this morning from the president of the coal company
instructing his general manager to discharge all employés whose
services were not absolutely needed, and to reduce expenses to
a minimum preparatory to a six-months' or a year's shut-down
of the coal mines here.

Succeeding this came a dispatch of August
28th, which said:

SPRING VALLEY, Ill., August 28.—[Special.] — The Spring
Valley Coal Company to-day discharged their entire general
office force for an indefinite period.   Every move that is made
is indicative of carrying out the order to close down the mine
for a year or six months.   The town is fast becoming deserted.

September 25th the offer of August 23d was
repeated in a long communication to the public,
printed in the appendix, through Governor
Fifer, and was accompanied by this solemn as-

severation: " It is all the concession we can possibly make to our men and maintain ourselves in a competitive market." If this were true, it would not excuse the company's treatment of the men. But it was not true, as your own spokesmen shall prove, and as can be shown by three business facts which the wayfaring man, though a fool, can read. At the very moment this statement was made a mine with precisely the same kind of veins, quality of coal, etc., as yours, that at Loceyville, four miles away, was at work, paying its miners the unreduced rate of wages you gave before your lock-out — 90 cents a ton — although it was far inferior in capital, equipment, etc., and so had to buy dearer and sell cheaper than you. That is fact number one. Fact number two is just as clear, and proves that the coal company's statement, in five columns of fine print, of September 25th (see appendix), was prepared to deceive the public and prevent them from learning the truth, that the lock-out was really an offensive movement of millionaires to put down the livelihood of poor men below the level paid by other mineowners, below the competitive level, below what you really could afford to pay, and below the cost of their subsistence. This fact, number two, was the resumption, close upon your statement, of the mines at La Salle and Peru, at prices more than double what you had offered August 23d, and had declared September 25th were all that could possibly be paid. These mines have the same coal and veins as yours, but nothing like your capital, equipment or market connections. Fact number three is strongest of all, and comes out of your own mouth. Within a month after declaring, on September 25th, that your offer of August 23d was all you could give and live, you of the coal company on October 24th, in the negotiations carried on by Rev. John F. Power, made your men an offer double that of August 23d, viz.: 82½ cents a ton, with an increase of brushing of only eight inches, instead of fourteen, and only two men in a room, instead of three. In fact, this offer was considerably more than double that which you had so formally and solemnly declared a month before was the best you could do and live. The increase of eight inches of brushing takes off about only 3 to 5 cents a ton from the offer, leaving about 77½ cents net, and you made some other concessions, allowing for which, makes the offer of October 24th considerably more than double the " last ditch " proposition of only four weeks before. The new offer was described in a press dispatch of October 24th, from Spring Valley, to the Chicago *Tribune*, as follows:

This afternoon the following telegram was received from the president of the coal company:

We are willing to pay 82½ cents per ton for screened coal and 70 cents per ton for run of the mine (rough and tumble); also twenty-four inches of brushing, with two men in a room and fourteen yards of coal face; no back rent to pay from May 1st to November 1st, but we shall insist upon contracts being signed, and no committees to treat with us. We are willing that the men shall have all the unions they wish independent of us.

Immediately upon the receipt of this, the secretary of the Miner's Union forwarded the following to the press:

WHY THE SPRING VALLEY MINERS WOULD NOT SIGN MR. SCOTT'S CONTRACT.

SPRING VALLEY, October 28.

Following are the resolutions adopted at a mass-meeting held the 26th inst. which had been called for the purpose of hearing read a proposed contract which was drafted by Manager Dalzell on the part of the company and James McNulty on the part of the miners. It had been agreed at a previous meeting by Mr. Dalzell and the miners, that, as the contract before submitted by the company was objectionable to the miners, that one be drafted as above, and Mr. Dalzell gave the miners to understand that the objectionable feature might be stricken out, but that was not done, and the rules submitted to the meeting for the approval of the miners were, with few exceptions, the original document. It appeared to the miners that undue advantage was sought on the part of the company, whereupon the following preamble and resolution was adopted:

WHEREAS, The locked-out miners of Spring Valley have used every endeavor to bring about a settlement, and have gone so far as to surrender some of their rights as American citizens; and,

WHEREAS, The terms offered the Spring Valley Coal Company — viz.: 82½ cents per ton, with twenty-four inches of brushing — gives it advantages over all the mines in the La Salle and other districts in northern Illinois; and

WHEREAS, The Spring Valley Coal Company has refused to start its mines on these conditions unless we would surrender the last vestige of our rights — the right of association; therefore be it

Resolved, That we the miners of Spring Valley, in mass-meeting assembled, do hereby rescind all former propositions to the company, and bind ourselves to accept no proposition except that already submitted — viz., 82½ cents per ton, twenty-four inches of brushing, working place of forty-two feet, with two men in a place; all other conditions the same as last year.

This offer of October 24th, the men were ready to accept had you not insisted that they should still surrender their unions and sign an iron-clad contract which bound them to all possible disadvantages and bound you to nothing. To save their union, without which they well know they will in the end lose everything that makes them free men, the miners kept up the forlorn struggle a few days longer. But it was hopeless. The importation of men from the Pennsylvania field was begun by the company, and threatened to fill the mines with outsiders,

False reports were sent out through the newspapers that the lock-out was settled at Spring
Valley, and in consequence miners began
flocking in and contributions for relief began to
slacken. The last day came, and the miners,
exhausted utterly, succumbed to the slow siege
of slander and starvation, and at a meeting on
November 12th, voted by secret ballot to give
up the struggle, to apply for work as " individuals," and sign the " contract" falsely so called,
which the company had drafted. The ranks
that had stood so heroically together for so
many months, broke. It was a race to see who
could get first to the office and enter servitude
on the Pennsylvania plan.

This offer by you of the coal company on
October 25th of more than double what you
had offered August 23d, and had declared,
September 25th, was all you could offer and
live, was an admission outright of the real purpose of your doings. It was a confession that
you had created, or allowed to be created, all-
the misery of Spring Valley to increase your
profits by cutting down the wages of your
men below what you and others were paying,
and could afford to pay. This is what your
long letters to the governor, statements to the
public and interviews in the papers boil down

to. All the clever columns of assorted statistics, mystifying talk about competitive fields,
railway discriminations, "junction points,"
jargon about "brushing" and slanderous
charges that the men would rather live on
charity than work, you having yourselves
taken away their work and made them beg-
gars — all simmer down to this: You made
commercial war on them, their wives and
children, to add to your millions at the risk of
misery, disease and death to them. The payment by the competitors all about you of double
what you offered, your own offer of double
what you repeatedly assured the public was all
you could pay, indicates your dreadful purpose to buy your brothers " below cost."

It was for this these poor men were seduced
into leaving homes and employment elsewhere
to settle in "your town;" that they were
snared in the meshes of land purchase on
monthly installments without a title, making
the purchase of a home a means of slavery
instead of the refuge and support it should be.
It was for this the labor market was over-
stocked by bringing in superfluous miners
from Belgium, France, Italy, and all parts of
America; that one-third of the mines were
shut down in December, and the rest in April,

without notice; that having promised " steady employment," your agent refused for five months to give the arbitrarily disemployed men any explanation or any chance to work at any price; that he then offered them less than half what neighboring mines, poorer than yours, are paying; that he refused to arbitrate; that he would not receive the men when they came offering to work at the prices paid elsewhere, which he had sworn in public you would pay and better; that he dragged the men about from conference to conference at La Salle and Joliet and Chicago for a compromise which he had no thought of making; that he demanded the abandonment of their union by men who, without union, were but brittle sticks to be broken by you one by one at your pleasure. It is for this that the homes of the poor have been broken up, and the men, leaving wives and children to face the terrors of starvation, have been driven forth in heartbreak to seek work where a million unemployed were tramping ahead of them.

CHAPTER VIII.

A " FREE " CONTRACT.

THE arrangements under which the miners went back to work for you are called " contracts."

It is of the essence of contracts that they should be free; and to be free, they must be the voluntary agreements of equal parties, made without duress, and with a full understanding of all the obligations assumed and imposed. The means taken by the " party of the first part " to prepare the minds and bodies of the " parties of the second part," at Spring Valley, to accept the terms of the iron-clad printed contract offered them, were of a kind not to be found recommended in any of the law books. They were such as these:

Months of disemployment and of intimidating; refusal to give explanations why work had been stopped or when it would be resumed; the application of the torture of famine and of compulsory exile; systematic slander and misrepresentation through public and private channels; threats that the idleness might be prolonged for years; the public and repeated menace that other workingmen would be brought in to take their livelihood away from them, by force, " If it takes all the power of the State to do it," said the figure-head of the millionaires ; the terrifying assertion that the pay was to be reduced from 90 cents to 35 cents a ton; threats of evictions and of forfeiture of all the earnings invested in the purchase of lots and building material bought from the company on the installment plan.

These were the influences used to prepare the men to make a " free " contract.

When the men broke their ranks, and ran to the company's office to " settle," they stood in a long file, hundreds of them passing one by one before the clerk's window to " sign." The paper given them, the " contract," was two pages, foolscap size, of fine print. They had no time to read it. Not one of them would have dared to ask to be allowed to read it before signing at the risk of finding his name on the black list when he came back. It would have done none of them any good if they had read it. They couldn't have understood its full scope, its provisions, carefully conned over by and woven together at their leisure by shrewd business men with the help of the best legal advice, embodying all the latest decisions of the courts in the phrasing of the different clauses. If they could have understood it, they couldn't have got it changed. Oliver Twist asking for " more " was nothing of a spectacle in comparison with a miner who should dream of suggesting some alterations to suit him in the " contract " he was about to sign. Imagine him, the " free " party of the second part, his clothes hanging limp over the cavities in his person caused by seven months enforced idleness, his wife and children at home waiting for what he will bring, the relief contributed by the public stopped by the news that work has begun. Imagine this " citizen " standing up to the five hundred million dollars which looks out at him over the counter through the supercilious eyes of the clerk. Try to fancy his saying : " This contract suits me, all but this and that ; make that so-and-so, and we will call it a bargain ! "

Of the men who scrambled over each other to get to the windows to " sign," a great many could not read at all ; a great many, being French, Belgian, Italian, German, Polish, could not read English. No one read the contract to them ; no one explained it. As fast as they could sign their names or make their mark, they passed on.

As each one came up he gave his name. The clerk, before presenting the " contract " for him to sign, it was observed, always glanced down to his desk. " What's your name? Brown?" Looks down. "That's all right, Brown; put your name here. Now, then, next!"

Here is one of the faithfulest members of the relief committee in the line. " What's your name? Bourke, you say? I'll see." Looks down. " B–B–B–Bourke. Ah! yes, Bourke. I haven't any contract for you. You will have to see the superintendent. Next."

It is the " black list "which lies on the clerk's desk. Bourke of the relief committee is on the list. He will get no work. He will have to go far from Spring Valley before his waiting wife and children get any earnings of his for the purchase of food He is a " free " man — free to leave, free to hunt work, free to go into exile.

Here is the so-called contract. It binds the company to nothing but that while it keeps the man at work it will pay him so much a ton. The miner is bound to work usually from May to May, in this case from December to May, but the company is not bound to give him work. The miner cannot discharge the company for any cause, but they may discharge him whenever they see fit. The miner makes his payment, which is in coal, to the company every day, but the company makes him wait two weeks to six weeks for every dollar it owes him. However starveling may be his wages, the miner has to bind himself to join no combination to better them. If he even smiles upon any such combination, it is under the penalty of losing all the company owes him for work, and the company is the judge whether or not he has smiled an insubordinate smile. Meanwhile, the company may join any conspiracy it chooses to put down the wages of the men, or put up the price of coal. If the pit boss is a tyrant, and oppresses the miner, as he has hundreds of ways of doing, the miner has the privilege under the " contract " of appealing for redress to this pit boss who has wronged him. The miner who knows that all of his associates have under compulsion signed away their right to defend him by the only power that could help him, the power of the union, and that he stands in the darkness of the pit simply as an individual, is not likely to antagonize the petty despot of the mines.

But if he has the rare courage to do so, and gets an adverse decision, he has one privilege more. He can appeal from the pit boss to the superintendent, whose appointee the pit boss is.

All of which amounts to this: that the miner, the weaker party, agrees to leave all disputed questions to the decision of the other party, opposed to him in interest at all points. No wonder the workingman has to be locked out and starved before he feels " free " enough (of food and manhood) to make such a bargain.

MINER'S ANNUAL CONTRACT.

THIS AGREEMENT, Made this......day of......A. D. 18.. Between THE SPRING VALLEY COAL COMPANY of the first part, and......of the second part.

Witnesseth, That the said party of the second part has agreed, and by these presents does hereby agree, to enter into the employment of the said party of the first part, as a miner of coal ......to commence on the......day of......A. D. 18.., and continue therein until the first day of May, A. D. 18.., and to abide by, adhere to and observe the rules and regulations set out and printed on the back hereof, numbered from one to eleven, inclusive, and which are hereby made a part of this contract, to the like extent as if herein written.

The party of the first part hereby agrees to pay the party of the second part, for each and every ton of screened coal mined by the party of the second part, delivered in pit cars at the face of the coal, after being weighed, passing over a screen, the bars of which shall not be more than seven-eighths (7/8) of an inch apart, as near as the same can be made, and the width and length of which shall not exceed the dimensions of the screens now in use by the party of the first part, the sum of......cents per ton of 2,000 pounds, and for each and every ton of 2,000 pounds of the run of the mine or for unscreened coal, the sum of......cents per ton of 2,000 pounds.

The said party of the second part further agrees to and with the party of the first part, that the price herein agreed to be paid by the party of the first part for all coal mined in the so-called Third Vein of the mines of the party of the first part, whether the same shall be screened or unscreened coal, shall be in full consideration to the said party of the second part for keeping his room, or working place, in good working order, including twenty-four (24) inches of brushing, which brushing must be done the full width of the roadways.

The said party of the second part further agrees to assist the pusher or driver employed by the party of the first part in starting the loaded cars from the face of the coal for such distance as may be necessary, provided such distance shall not exceed ten (10) yards ; also, to take the empty cars from the first parting or switch, to the face of the coal.

The said party of the first part hereby reserves the right and privilege, however, of closing the mines at any time, and of discharging any miner for cause, including the party of the second part, as the superintendent, or person in charge of the mine for the time being may think proper ; but the party of the first part agrees that in case steady and continuous work cannot be furnished the party of the second part during the life of this agreement, that such work as may have to be done, shall be fairly divided with and apportioned to said party of the second part, on the basis of all the men so employed at and during such time. All payments hereunder to be made monthly on regular pay day, and in compliance with the rules and regulations above named, and pay day is hereby fixed for and on the Saturday nearest to the 15th day of each month, when and at which time all wages or moneys that may have been earned during and in the calendar month next prior to such pay day shall be paid, less all moneys owing said party of the first part on any account whatever.

It is hereby expressly agreed and understood by the party of the second part, that should he become a tenant of the party of

8

the first part during the term of his engagement, then in case of the termination of this contract, either by his discharge from the employ of said first party, or in any other way, the term of such tenancy shall at once cease and be determined without notice, and he will vacate the premises so occupied by him, upon verbal notice of the agent or superintendent of said first party, written notice to quit being hereby expressly waived, and on failure so to do shall be deemed guilty of a forcible detainer of such premises, and that he will not be entitled to demand or receive any part of the wages due him for labor performed (should the party of the first part so elect) until such premises are vacated, and the keys thereof delivered at the office of the said first party.

And the party of the second part further agrees that he will not stop work, leave the employment of the said party of the first part, or join or become a party to, either directly or indirectly, any strike or combination for the purpose of obtaining, or the intent of which is to obtain from, or cause the company, party of the first part, to pay their miners an advance of wages, or pay beyond what is specified in this contract. Nor will he in any manner aid, abet or countenance any such strike, combination or scheme whatever, which has for its purpose any such object or design, during the time specified in the first clause of this contract. And if the said party of the second part at any time shall violate any of the provisions of this contract in this regard, he shall thereby forfeit all claim for coal prior thereto mined and not paid for, and the said first party shall be fully released from all liability on account of this contract, or any labor performed by the said party of the second part.

In Witness Whereof, the said parties have hereunto set their hands and seals, the day and year first above written.

THE SPRING VALLEY COAL COMPANY.

By....................................[SEAL.]
Agent and Superintendent.

....

Witness:
..........................[SEAL.]

(SIGNED IN DUPLICATE.)

☞ *Read the Rules and Regulations on the Other Side.*

RULES AND REGULATIONS OF THE SPRING VALLEY COAL
COMPANY.

Adopted for the Purpose of Regulating Mining and Other Employment in and About their Coal Mines.

I.—Every employé of the Company will be required to be
ready for duty when the whistle blows for work, every morning,
and will be expected to perform a full day's work in his respective line of employment, unless the foreman of his department
orders less time to be worked. Engineers are strictly forbidden
to lower any miner or underground laborer into any pit after 7
o'clock a. m., without orders from the Pit-Boss or person in
charge of the pit head.

II.—No suspension of work shall take place during working
hours, except in case of actual necessity ; nor shall any miner be
absent from his work during working hours without leave from
the Pit-Boss, except in case of sickness or other unavoidable
contingency that would prevent him from working.

III.—Any employé feeling aggrieved in any respect, must
present his claim to the Pit-Boss in person. If they fail to ad-
just the matter in a manner satisfactory to the employé, it may
be referred to the Superintendent (if either party desires), whose
decision, upon the hearing of both sides of the question, will be
final. In case, however, the complaint arises from personal
grounds between the Pit-Boss and the miner, the Superintendent, at his option, may change the miner to some other shaft.

IV.—Any employé who may have been discharged by the
Company, or who, with the consent of the Company, may have
left its service, shall receive all arrearages of pay due him at
once. The Company will consent to their employés leaving their
service without previous notice, provided such employé has conformed to the terms and conditions of this contract with the
party of the first part, and the rules and regulations governing
the working of the mines.

V.—No person will be allowed to interfere in any manner
with the employer's just right of employing, retaining and discharging from employment, any person or persons whom the

Superintendent or Pit-Boss having charge of the mines for the time being may consider proper; nor interfere in any way, by threats and menace, or otherwise, with the right of any employé to work, or engage to work in any way, and upon any terms, and with whom he may think proper and best for his interest, or the benefit of his family.

VI.--No employé will be permitted to fill his place by another man without the consent of the Superintendent.

VII.—Every employé will be paid once a month at regular pay day, all wages or moneys he may have earned during and in the calendar month next prior to such pay day, after deducting any indebtedness which such employé may owe to the Company, or which the Company, with the consent of such employé, may have assumed to pay to any other person.

VIII.—On the side where coal is not mined in a miner's place, the corner of the wall shall not be more than three (3) feet from the face of the coal, and shall extend six (6) feet from the corner along the face. The gob wall must not be over five (5) feet from the face, and must extend six (6) feet from the pack. On the side where coal is mined, the corner of the pack must not be over two (2) feet from the face of the coal; the pack and gob to be built in the same manner as above; the pack and road walls to be built of brushing rock only; the gob and packs to be built to the roof. It shall be the duty of every miner working in the mines, provided there is a sufficient supply of props, as required by law, to keep his room or working place in said mines in good order and repair, as specified above; and any such miner who shall willfully, carelessly, or negligently suffer them to get out of such order or repair, as above specified, and who shall not upon request immediately put the same in repair in the manner required by these rules, the Company may put such places in repair at the expense of the miner in default, and may retain the amount of such expense from the next or any future payment to which said employé would otherwise be entitled, until fully reimbursed for such expense. And in case a room or working place should close, when the miner has complied with the above requirements, then it shall be the duty of the Company to put the same in good order and repair at its own expense ; if it is found impossible to stow all rock in the gob and a part must be loaded and sent out, the part sent out must be fire-clay, and not brushing rock.

IX.—No miner who has left the employment of the Company, whether voluntarily or by discharge, will be entitled to receive any arrearages of pay due him for labor performed, whether on the regular pay day or during the interval preceding pay, until he shall have put his room or working place in perfect working order, as required by his contract with the Company. All miners leaving said employment will be required to procure the certificate of the Pit-Boss that they have complied with the requirements of this rule, as aforesaid, before making application at the Company's office for final payment.

X.—Any tenant of the Company, upon leaving its service, whether voluntarily or by discharge, will not be entitled to receive any part of the wages due him for labor performed, until he shall have vacated the premises occupied by him (should the Superintendent or other person in charge of the mines for the time being so elect), and presented the keys of the same at the office.

XI.—The miners may, at their option and expense, employ a Check Weighman, whose duties shall be to see that the coal is weighed correctly by the weighman employed by the Company ; provided that the party so employed shall be a miner in the employment of this Company, and in good standing at the time he may be selected for the position.

Under this contract a man may forfeit his pay for the whole of one month, and up to the third Saturday of the next month. The company makes the law, and is the sole judge and executioner, allowing no appeal.

The third of the rules which form a part of the contract makes the miner who feels aggrieved appeal " in person " to the pit boss. When the men's union was recognized, their remedy was quite different; much more likely to preserve the rights of the weaker party. Under the union, the miners, when aggrieved, made their complaints to a committee of their own number, called the pit committee. This committee stood between the boss and the complainant, and behind the committee stood the union of all the men. The difference between this kind of a hearing and that when the miner stands alone, with nobody behind him, and asks for justice from the pit boss, behind whom stands $500,000,-000 and the power of dismissal, eviction, banishment and the black list, does not need to be pointed out.

Only the company's pleasure limits the company's power under these rules to forfeit any arrearages of pay due the miner if he leaves before the end of the year for which he has signed. No matter how extreme may be the emergency which calls him away, if the company chooses to say no to his application for release, he can only go by breaking his contract. If he breaks his contract he may lose as much as six weeks' wages, or about one-sixth of the actual income of the year. If he

must go, and the company chooses to force
him to break the contract, he has no redress;
its decision is supreme.

The possibilities of putting extra work and
expense on the miner, under the eighth and
ninth rules, are limitless. The pit boss is the
sole judge. When the union was the medi-
ator between the company and the organized
men, the company would never attempt to
shift the " deadwork " of the mine on the men,
unless it wanted to precipitate a strike by the
whole body. Now that no power can inter-
vene, the company has but to say to the miner,
Do this, Do that, and he must submit. There
has been a steady increase year by year in the
amount of labor on the roadways, and other
deadwork once paid for, which the company
is requiring the men to do without compensation. The company used to pay for all the
" brushing;" it now compels the miners to do
twenty-four inches of it without pay. This
shifting of burdens will be accelerated since
the union has been ruined. The men who
must do so much more unremunerated work
in making the roadways, taking out the rock,
etc., will have proportionately less time for
earning money by mining coal.

This " free " contract puts the workingman

under a yearly bond.   It makes him agree to
abide for a year by a scale of wages fixed as
summer, the dull season, is coming on.   The
winter is over.   The demand for coal in May
is at its minimum.   Prices of coal are at their
lowest, and the wages for the whole year are
made proportionate to this ebb-tide price.
The yearly bond of the contract says to the
miner: You must forego any advantage that
might come to you in the more active months
of the year.   If supply and demand vary, you
are not to profit by it.   No matter how high
coal goes, nor how much our profits increase,
you must remain bound to work for this
minimum wage.   We may " strike " the public
every week for higher prices; you must agree
for a full year not to strike for any change in
wages.   And by the ingenious system of keeping back each month's pay until the middle of
the next month, the employers always have on
hand at least one twenty-fourth of the miner's
whole annual income, to be forfeited if he talks
even in his sleep about asking for " more."   If
these are free contracts, it is a singular thing
that it should be so difficult to get the miners
to make them.   They protest against them in all
their conventions and conferences.   After six
months of idleness and famine at Spring Valley,

the men stood out four weeks longer in their misery, and that of their families, in the hope that they might escape the " free contract." They were whipped into signing it, just as truly as the Southern slave was whipped to his tasks, and more cruelly.

The bald truth is that this yearly contract is slavery. It is slavery in yearly installments. Put together, year by year, it is a slavery for life. The miners, in submitting to it, and we, in allowing them to submit to it, degrade their manhood, and that of the republic. Slavery, in no matter how small a spot, among a free people, is like a spark in a cargo of cotton, a leak in a ship. It cannot be so insignificant that it does not imperil the whole. The miners, to a man, ought to resist this slavery, and the public should sustain them in doing so at any cost. Relief given these men in such a struggle would not be " charity ; " it would be an investment for the defense of the liberties and the homes of the whole people, all of which are in peril, if any are in peril. Our forefathers had the wit to see and act on this wise scheme of mutual self-interest ; have not we ? Our constitutions, laws, revenues, expenditures, public policies at home and abroad, are all operated by the help of the votes of workingmen who

are thus subjugated all over the country to
the will of the lords of industry.   Are these
votes likely to go to the benefit of the public
which unconcernedly sees them denied their
rights, or to the benefit of those who hold them
under the yoke ?

Spring Valley at the city election in April,
1889, cast 949 votes.

The poison of these servitudes among the
people works up and back into the liberties of
the rest of us just as surely as the pestilence of
the slums creeps through the drainage of the
city into the palace.

In defense of these contracts, it was urged
by a newspaper at the county seat, the Prince-
ton *Tribune*, that under them the miners " bind
themselves to work until May 1st, just as the
company binds itself to furnish a certain
amount of coal " to railroads " at a stipulated
price, until May." The comparison would
compare if the railroad got its contracts for
fuel out of the coal company by refusing it all
transportation at any price, as the coal company refused its miners work, until it surrendered and " signed." No court would uphold
such a compulsory arrangement as a contract,
and the workingmen ought to have the same

rights to protection under the law of contract that the rich have.

Such arrangements are not contracts. They are servitudes, imposed by force and fraud upon those who do not consent, but submit by compulsion. The interesting question forces itself at once to the front whether, if the miners have not been working under contract, they are bound to treat the wages they have received as payment in full. They have against those who have taken the proceeds of their labor a valid and ought-to-be legal claim for the unpaid difference between what they have received and what they ought to have received. The enforcement of these claims will be perfectly feasible the moment the people make themselves really what they are now theoretically, their own rulers, and have in the courts, legislature and executive chambers servants who will work for the people instead of doing tricks for privilege. If the millennial day ever comes when those unjust men are mulcted to restore to the people what they have filched from them, they will deserve no pity. The penalty will be a light one for their offense in playing a false part, betraying those who trusted them. If they want to make contracts that will hold both sides, let them make contracts that are contracts.   The courts are every day releasing business men from contracts that are held to be no contracts, because of misunderstanding, inadequate value given, improper pressure, duress, variance with public policy, and so on indefinitely.   Is this law of contract for a class only?   Are only the well-to-do and the strong to have the aid of the courts?

CHAPTER IX.

APPEALING TO THE GOVERNOR.

WHEN you of the Spring Valley Coal Company broke silence after the lock-out had lasted more than five months, and made your intimidating offer of thirty-five cents a ton, as explained in full in the preceding chapter, the city officials, business men and miners of Spring Valley made the following appeals to the governor of Illinois:

SPRING VALLEY, September 9, 1889.

To the Hon. Joseph Fifer, Governor of Illinois.

SIR—We, the Mayor and Common Council of the City of Spring Valley, and the coal miners and business men of Spring Valley, desire to submit for your consideration a few facts concerning the mining industry in this valley.

Spring Valley is the center of a mining area of 40,000 acres of the best coal lands in Illinois. The Spring Valley Coal Company owns the coal rights in this vast tract of land. The town site of the city of Spring Valley was also owned by a Town Site Company, controlled by the coal company, but it has been sold at high prices to persons settling in the city. There were four mining plants operated here by the coal company until December, 1888. The company owns most of the houses occupied by the miners, and runs a "Company Store," at which they are to trade. Coal mining is the only industry on which the town depends for existence, there being no factories and no stores save such as deal in supplies to the community.

On December, 1888, shafts Nos. 2 and 4 were shut down, throwing out of work about 1,000 men. Their comrades, knowing that the men and their families thus turned into unexpected idleness in the dead of winter, would starve, divided their own work with them. For the rest of the winter every miner laid off one day in three in order to give part work to all. This lasted into April. Then the community, exhausted by the strain of supporting three men and their families on the earnings of two men, received its final blow. April 29th, without previous notice of any kind, all the miners were told to take out their tools and leave the mines, which they did. In one afternoon their livelihood was taken from them, and since then no work has been done in the Spring Valley mines.

The results are these: The entire mining population here is without work, without income, without food enough to maintain a bare existence, and without clothing and fuel to meet the approaching fall and winter. Women and children are sick and without medical attendance, medicines, nourishing food or proper nursing. Wet weather is coming, to be followed by cold, and our people can no longer go barefoot, unclad and ill-fed, as they have been doing. Hence our needs demand prompt and vigorous attention.

According to the company's officials, the men, when mining, receive $43 a month each on the average. According to the men, the average wage per month was about $30 each. This was when ninety cents per ton was the rate paid for mining. The Spring Valley Coal Company, some time since proposed a reduction in wages equivalent to about fifty-five cents per ton. In detail the proposition was this; First, to reduce the rate from ninety cents per ton seventy-five cents—being fifteen cents per ton off; second, the men to do thirty inches of "brushing" instead of sixteen inches, as formerly, being fourteen inches brushing additional, equivalent to ten cents per ton reduction; and lastly, three men to work where two had formerly been employed—a proposition in itself involving a loss of nearly one-third the earnings of each man. The whole reduction by this proposition would be not less than fifty-five cents per ton. Whether the men, when working at ninety cents per ton, got $43 per month, as figured by the company, or $30 per month as figured by the men, it is apparent at once that the proposed reduction of fifty-five cents per ton would reduce their wages more than one-half, or from $43 to about $20, or from $30 to about $14 per month. Ordinary intelligence suffices to show the impossibility of a family living on from $14 to $20 a month.

It is to be remarked here, that, while these heavy reductions in wages were proposed, no suggestion of reducing the rents of miners living in company houses, was made; nor were any reductions made in the prices of coal or of goods sold miners at the company's store. On the contrary, on the 18th of July, the miners, being unable to pay their rent, were served with five-day notices that their rent was in arrear, and "that in default of the payment by them of the rent so due within the time aforesaid, their right to occupy said premises would cease, and proceedings would be instituted for the recovery of the possession of said premises in pursuance of the statute of this State. (Signed) The Spring Valley Coal Company."

We most respectfully point out to you that the men at Spring Valley are not strikers, but are the victims of two lock-outs, one last December and the other in April last. We point out, too, that the men came here on invitation of the company, and many have bought or built homes expecting to have work with which to support their families and to pay the mortgages they were compelled to assume in order to secure their homes. Instead of work and wages, however, they have had months of enforced idleness and starvation, and the city and mines of Spring Valley have been virtually abandoned by the men who promoted the Spring Valley Company, and who laid out this city and induced the people to come here to settle. We ask: Is it right for capitalists to buy up thousands of acres of land, lay out towns, open mines, employ thousands of laborers, and induce many thousands more to settle in their towns in the expectation of work, and then to shut down the mines, stop wages, and drive an entire community to idleness and destitution? Is this right? Do the people of Illinois sanction industrial organization and business methods such as these?

Again we were told in the fall of 1888 that the success of the ticket on which you were nominated for governor meant work and wages. The presidential campaign in 1888 was fought with appeals to workmen and promises of prosperity.

Where, we ask, is the prosperity promised us? It is proper to point out in this connection that we are reduced to a condition of destitution, notwithstanding these promises. Such being the condition, we ask you to consider the situation and to devise such measures for the relief of the miners as to you seem proper. We would suggest:

1. A proclamation calling our needs to the attention of the people of the entire State, and asking contributions of food, clothing and money, and pointing out that, while some of the mining difficulties have been settled, those in Spring Valley yet remain. It should be emphasized that the settlement of strikes elsewhere in the coal region has caused the public to slacken in their contributions for relief in the mistaken belief that the Spring Valley difficulty was included in the agreement. This is an error. The men are still out of work, and the situation at Spring Valley is worse than it has been elsewhere.

2. Place the adjutant-general of the State in charge of a suitable organization for the collection and distribution of the food and clothing needed here.

3. Recognize the situation of the Spring Valley miners as an emergency demanding instant action on your part to relieve the people, and use for that purpose any special fund of money at your disposal. Surely there must be means within your control to meet such an emergency.

4. Come to Spring Valley and personally investigate the needs of the people here, and supervise the measures you inaugurate for their relief. The devastation of the flood at Johnstown induced Governor Beaver of Pennsylvania to give his personal attention to the relief of the sufferers there, and it is pertinent to ask whether a community of 5,000 persons in Illinois

in the throes of starvation for months is not a catastrophe demanding as prompt and thorough action from the government and the people as the disaster at Johnstown.   The people at Johnstown were drowned.   Here are living victims to starvation.   We ask, therefore, that you will personally inspect this battle of 5,000 miners with destitution; and we believe it will spur you to instant action.

5. Finally we ask you to submit to the Legislature, which should be convened in special session, an inquiry into the condition of the coal industry in this State, to the end that legislation may be framed adequate to afford permanent relief for the laboring masses engaged in that industry.

Respectfully submitted,

H. DUGGAN,
Mayor of Spring Valley.

CONNOR KELLY,
PATRICK FLOOD,
THOS. LINSLEY,
PATRICK J. O'BRIEN,
JOSEPH ROBERTS,
THOS. GAVIN,
WILLIAM PROCTOR,
V. H. WEISSENBERGER,
Aldermen of Spring Valley.

SPRING VALLEY MINERS, IN MASS MEETING ASSEMBLED: By,

A. D. BOURKE, President.
THOMAS BRADY, Secretary.
M. J. COVENY, M. D.
H. ROEDERER, Baker.
J. H. STEADMAN, Butcher.
W. J. NOLAN, Grocer.
JAN BUDNIK, Saloon.
J. HERCER, Mang. Co-oper. Store.
JOS. SALZER, Dry Goods.
MICHAEL STANTON, City Clerk.

The business men's letter was as follows:

SPRING VALLEY, ILL., Sept. 10, '89.

To the Hon. Joseph Fifer, Governor of Illinois.

SIR—We, the undersigned business men of Spring Valley, respectfully represent that we came to the city of Spring Valley and invested our means in business here relying upon the promises and prospects of the Spring Valley Coal Company to do a large coal mining business—such a business, in fact, as would employ large numbers of miners and laborers, who, with their wages, could buy our goods and maintain our establishments.

We further represent that for nearly five months past the mines in Spring Valley have been shut down, and the working-men of this city to the number of nearly 2,500 have been out of work and out of wages with which to buy our goods.

The result of this is that our business is prostrate, and must continue prostrate until the miners are given work and are put in position to buy goods as formerly.

If the present state of affairs continues, the business men of this city will be driven out of business by insolvency and almost complete loss of trade.

We, therefore, earnestly ask of you a personal investigation of the mining difficulties in this place, and that you take all measures in your power to effect an early settlement of these troubles and the resumption of work in the Spring Valley mines.   Respectfully submitted,

BERKSTRESSER & PORTERFIELD, Grocers; R. D. BUCHAN, Clothing, etc.; JAMES THOM, General Merchant; JOHN A. BURCHAM, Glassware; F. E. MASON & Co., Agricultural Imp.; G. E. REED, Furniture; J. C. SITTERLY, Livery; A. A. CADY, Grocery; WM. ANDREW SMITH, News Depot; J. C. PINKLEY, Druggist; G. M. BUTTS, Boots and Shoes; JOHN SOLANN, Saloon; JAMES POWERS, Grocer; THOS. CHEESEMAN, Jeweler; GEORGE HOFFMAN, Bakery; E. G. THOMPSON, Druggist; JOHN FOESTER, Boots and Shoes: JOHN DONLAN, Shoes and Boots; S. M. HORNER, Hotel; T. C. KOHN, Principal of Schools; JACOB WAHL, Saloon; JOHN MCMAHON, Sample Room; MRS.

A. DAVIS, Confectionery; J. J. OSBORNE, Hotel and Restaurant; STANTON BROS., Sample Room; JOS. NIEMSHIK, Cigarmaker; WM. KLINGBERG, Merchant Tailor; J. J. CALLAHAN, Clothier; MRS. R. HEEP, Hardware, etc.; BERNARDO PERADOTTA, Saloon; MARTIN DELMAGRO, Groceries; I. J. JAGODZINSKI, Grocery; JOSEPH RIVA, Grocery; L. FRANK, Clothing. HENNEBRY BROS., Clothing; JOS. SALZER, Dry Goods; JOHN PICK, Sample Room; W. M. MURRAY, Drugs; M. SLOWEY, Groceries. GEO. SITTLER, Sample Room; P. KELLEY, Sample Room; JAMES HICKS, Sample Room; JOHN DIESBECK, Sample Room; L. R. DEAN, Furniture.

An anxious article on " The Present Situation," in the Spring Valley *Gazette* of May 1st of this year, shows that both the business men and the miners have reason to fear that " the ruling powers" intend to carry the Dooming of the Town into another twelvemonth to force another cut in wages. The 1st of May is the day for making the contract for wages for the year, but when " his" men try to find their Captain of Industry they can only learn that he has gone east " on business." What is to become of them is evidently no business of his. The *Gazette* says:

The 1st of May has arrived, and what will be done remains still unsolved. Last Friday afternoon a petition was signed by several hundred of the miners, and forwarded to the head of the company, asking him to come out here to try to effect a settlement. A petition was circulated among the business men indorsing the miners' request. They have received replies that he is east on business, and will not be back until about May 15th.

At the same meeting wherein the foregoing

memorial was adopted, the following resolutions were also offered and unanimously adopted by the miners:

WHEREAS, The proposition made to reduce our wages is both unjust and unreasonable, as we could not make a bare subsistence by the hardest work on the terms offered; and

WHEREAS, It has been sufficiently demonstrated that there is no reason or necessity for such a great reduction as that which the company offers. Therefore, be it

Resolved, That we decline to accept the proposition of fifteen cents a ton of a reduction, with other terms which will aggregate fifty-five cents per ton of reduction. Be it further

Resolved, That we are ready and willing to resume work on the conditions governing the settlement at Streator and other places in this district where a settlement has been made, namely, seven and one-half cents per ton of a reduction and last year's conditions.

On motion, Messrs. Brady, O'Hare and Gilletsky were appointed to see Mr. Dalzell and report the above resolutions. His reply to the committee was that he would not treat with any committee or recognize any organization; that he would treat with the men individually.

Commenting on this, the Chicago *Daily News* of September 13th said:

The appeal of the locked-out miners of Spring Valley to Governor Fifer, is deserving of the prompt attention of that public officer. The plain statement of the cruel treatment which they have received from the Spring Valley Coal Company, must arouse indignation in every mind. The company built a city, selling much of the property at a large profit to merchants and miners, whom it induced to settle there. The one reliance of the city was on the mines. 5,000 miners went thither under the

promise of obtaining work. Now the mines have been shut
down, and Spring Valley is ruined.

These locked-out miners deserve the help of the State and of
all the citizens. They have not struck for higher wages or even
against a reduction of their wages. They have been betrayed
by a soulless corporation and left to starve. By the authorita-
tive action of the governor, this infamous crime against labor
should be branded publicly. At the same time the victims
should be rescued from starvation.

The people of Spring Valley must be given help. A rich
man has sinned against them. Let the rich now relieve their
wants.

Instead of going in person, in response to
the appeals of the people of Spring Valley,
Governor Fifer sent his adjutant-general to
Spring Valley to investigate, and gave the
matter afterward no further attention.

The report made to Governor Fifer by Adjutant-General Vance of his investigation is one
of the curiosities of the literature of American
self-government. If such callousness to the
sufferings of the people, such undisguised
anxiety to shield members of an upper class
from the exposure of their misdeeds, such
cynical contempt for their victims, had been
exhibited by an agent of the French court of
Louis XVI. sent into the provinces before
1789, to investigate the reports of a distress
among the tenants of the seigneurs, it would
have excited little surprise, although it would
certainly have figured in the pages of Taine as

a supreme illustration of the cruelty of *l'ancien régime*. But when such a document comes, cold and calculated, from the official representative of a free American commonwealth, we can only lose ourselves in puzzling out what poisonous influences they may be which in one century have made it possible for a public servant to put forth, and the public to receive, utterances so completely hostile to all the sacredest principles and sympathies of republican democratic liberty and happiness. The legend of Marie Antoinette's inquiry why the poor of Paris did not eat cake, since they could not get bread, is well matched by Adjutant-General Vance's report at Spring Valley. " There is a general paralyzation of all business interests and trades, *except those* dealing in luxuries." The hardness of heart which could throw a taunt of this kind, officially, at a people suffering as bitterly as the evidence from all sides given heretofore proves that Spring Valley was, is an infallible index of a want of hardness of head.

Adjutant-General Vance was not happy in the task set him of making an investigation of the state of affairs at Spring Valley. His true place was that which he filled during the summer, when, at the head of the State militia, with loaded guns and fixed bayonets, he marched and countermarched through the towns of the coal regions, by order of Governor Fifer, for a chance to shoot working-men. The report of Adjutant-General Vance is as follows:

To His Excellency, Joseph W. Fifer, Governor of Illinois.

SIR—In compliance with your instructions, I proceeded to Spring Valley on the 17th inst., arriving there at 9 o'clock p. m. On the morning of the 18th I called upon Mayor Duggan, and informed him that I had been sent by your Excellency to ascertain the exact condition and to verify by personal observation the representations made to you as to the suffering condition of the people at Spring Valley. During the day the opportunity was afforded me to meet and converse with a large number of citizens upon the situation and to ascertain their views in reference to the alleged suffering in Spring Valley. My inquiries were more particularly made with a view to ascertain the condition as to the destitution, starvation, suffering, sickness, and general sanitary condition. I requested the mayor to point out the most prominent cases of destitution, or to have the supervisor of the township, who is ex-officio overseer of the poor, do so, as I would prefer to base my representation of the situation to you upon personal observation. The citizens with whom I conversed were representative of the population of Spring Valley, and included physicians, druggists, police, butchers, mechanics, miners, merchants, professional men, and business men generally.

The general sentiment expressed by these persons was that the memorial presented to you, and signed by many of them, was a misrepresentation as to the condition in reference to destitution, starvation, suffering, and sickness; that without any consultation or concert of action on their part, the memorial was prepared and submitted to them for signature. Some persons said they were opposed to the memorial as a whole;

that no such a condition existed as was represented; that there was no starvation, destitution, or sickness worthy of mention, but that they had signed the memorial because, if they refused to do so, they would be boycotted in business. Others seemed to take a different view. While they freely admitted the exaggerations in reference to starvation and destitution, yet they urged that there had been a necessity for charitable work, and that this necessity would probably exist for several weeks after the miners have resumed operations.

Physicians stated that there was very little sickness at this time, and their business was much lighter than usual at this season of the year; their cases were mostly of a malarial character, and only six cases of diphtheria in a mild form were under treatment when I left Spring Valley. Druggists stated that they had fewer requests for medicine from persons unable to pay for it than at any time for several years, and in no instance had they refused drugs to persons unable to pay for them. There is evidence of a sentiment of hostility toward both mine-owners and miners among citizens not engaged in these pursuits, for the reason, as stated by them, that neither of the above classes at Spring Valley seem to have made much effort to come to an agreement or to compromise their differences. There is a universal expression that the offer of 75 cents per ton for mining* and thirty inches of brushing with three men in a room would be unreasonable, and an unfair remuneration to the miners, and the company is charged with insincerity in making the offer. There is an equally strong conviction upon the part of many who should be competent to judge that the mines cannot be operated profitably at the prices demanded, and that men living upon charity should show a disposition to concede and a willingness to compromise out of the present difficulties. There is a growing sentiment there that men who will live upon the charity of a generous public rather than to work even at wages they deem inadequate for their own support are unworthy of the sympathy bestowed upon them.

---

* Equal to 35 cents a ton net.

From the best information I can obtain and from personal observation, I do not believe the population of Spring Valley will exceed 2,500 persons at this time.   There is a general paralyzation of all business interests and trades, except those dealing in luxuries.

Nineteen licensed saloons are doing business at this time, and are apparently well patronized * notwithstanding the depression in business generally.   At Spring Valley there are three veins of coal; the upper and lower veins are about three and one-half feet in thickness; the mining is done by hand, and is paid for by the ton.   The middle vein, ranging from four to six feet, with an average thickness of over five feet, is mined with machines, and the men operating them are paid by the day. There is apparently a strong prejudice existing between the men working in the middle vein and those working the other veins. The men working the middle vein did not cease working last May, because there was no reduction of their wages, and because they were satisfied; but the men operating the other veins demanded of them to quit work in sympathy with and in support of their contest with the company, which was refused. Since then the men working the middle vein have been termed "blacklegs" by the others.   The relief committee of the miners' union is at this time composed of fourteen persons, with representatives from each nationality.   Mr. Hill is president, Mr. Brady secretary, and Mr. McNulty treasurer.   I was informed by this committee that it met every morning at ten o'clock.   All cases of suffering and sickness are reported at this meeting. The committee informed me that it furnished medicines and delicacies for sick persons, or the money for their purchase when

* L. W. B., the very intelligent correspondent of the Chicago *Inter Ocean*, fast and faithful organ of the State Government General Vance represents, was at Spring Valley a few days before the adjutant-general.   Here is what he says about the saloons which General Vance declared to be so "well patronized:"

THE PLACE IS ABSOLUTELY DEAD.

Even the saloons are quiet.   There were forty-three of these before the lock-out.   There are now only nineteen, and they are quiet as the grave, except one near the hotel.   I heard a good deal of noise in this one, but found that the merrymakers were some young men who are clerks in the company's offices.   No one else has money to spend.

they were supplied with funds. The committee informed me that they issue provisions every Saturday from their supply store. The issues are made upon the basis of a value of 21 cents to the head of a family and 14 cents each for the women and children. This committee commenced receiving money and relief supplies May 29th, and had received in cash up to September 19th, $2,368.67. Cash on hand that date, $239.31. The supplies reported received are from miscellaneous sources to the value of about $800; three car-loads of provisions from Chicago, valued at about $1,000 each, two car-loads from Peoria; from Sheffield, one ton of flour and other supplies; from Chicago, four barrels of meat and fifteen barrels of flour. The committee reports that they are supplying aid to 405 heads of families; the total number of persons is 1.704, of whom there are 901 English speaking, 189 Poles, 339 French, 93 Germans, 101 Italians, and 72 Swedes. The committee states that these persons will not be self-supporting for at least one month after the mines resume operations. There are at least 200 of the miners that live at Spring Valley who are working at Loceyville, Ladd, and other points, all within a few miles of Spring Valley. This committee states that it has (except to six persons) refused to issue supplies to those who work in the middle vein, for the reason that they do not think they need relief.

The relief committee denies that it has advised men not to go elsewhere for work as a committee, and that, if advice of this kind has been given, it has been by individuals of their own volition. From the best information I could get from the citizens and relief committee, I do not believe there are to exceed 250 idle miners in Spring Valley at this time. Advertisements are posted in Spring Valley calling for 500 miners at Streator; fifty at Youngstown, Ohio; 200 at Centerville, Iowa, and sixty at Sandoval, Ill. An agent of the last-named company was in Spring Valley, but could secure no men. I have seen a letter from the office of the Secretary of the Miners' Union at Spring Valley to the Chenoa Coal Company which says: " Now, if you would guarantee me that men could make $2.50 per day, or you make them up to that, I would send you twenty-five good men,

if you would build them houses to live in, as all the single men
is about out of here.   There is agents here every day paying
men's fare to go to all parts of the country to dig coal, so you
see it will be hard to get men if they can't make $2.25 or $2.50
per day."

In the above I have given you an accurate report of the ex-
pressions and views of others, and of the situation as I found it.
I believe that there should be an organized system of relief
established by the citizens of Spring Valley outside of those engaged in the mining industry, for the benefit of women, children,
and sick persons only, and continued until the necessity for organized charity had ceased.   I ascertained that there had been
no action taken by the township or county authorities in their
official capacity to relieve any want and destitution that may
have existed.   Respectfully submitted.

JOSEPH W. VANCE, Adjutant General.

The slur about the miners preferring to live
on charity instead of work is paraded with
an eagerness which blinds the " general" to
the fact that his own statement further along
that " there are not 250 idle miners in Spring
Valley," where there had been 2,500, proves
that these people did not prefer charity to
work.   He pauses with evident relish on the
statement " that nineteen licensed saloons are
doing business at this time, and apparently
well patronized."   His anxiety to defend the
cruel oppressions of the people by showing
that the wretchedness is due to the viciousness
of the poor prevents him from seeing that he
has himself furnished the disproof of his own

statement.   It is impossible that 250 miners, idle ones at that, should be able to keep nineteen saloons "apparently well patronized." The report is couched throughout in language studiously calculated by such phrases as those about preferring charity to work, the prosperity of dealers in luxuries, the extensive patronage of the nineteen saloons by the 250 impecunious miners, the non-existence of the alleged destitution, and so forth, to create the impression that Spring Valley had no grievances but its own wickednesses, and no need of other relief than reform.   But the lack of head again upset the structure of the lacking heart by concluding with a recommendation for an organized system of relief to be " established by the citizens of Spring Valley, outside of those engaged in the mining industry." This recommendation is made apparently for the sole purpose of implying a slander against the Miners' Relief Committee, against whom no open charges are attempted to be brought, but its only effect was to undo all the elaborate effort of the preceding parts of the report to show that no need of relief existed.

This report throws no light on the condition of affairs at Spring Valley.   Any intelligent reader can make from the evidence given in this book a much clearer and fairer statement. But that such a document, in face of all the facts, should have been submitted to the governor by a high official of the State, should have been received by him, and without rebuke or correction, despite its open inconsistencies of statement and ugliness of temper, should have been given to the public as the only contribution the representatives of the people could or would make to the relief of Spring Valley, is a social fact of immense import.   It shows how high class hatred runs between the rich and the people in America. It shows that the downfall of the republic has gone so far that the people have lost their hold on their rulers.   These are not afraid to flaunt openly their contempt of the people, and to display unreservedly their subservience to the real power that governs the American people—the money power —the power of the few comparatively millionaires and corporations who do the thinking and leading in courts, markets and legislatures for the 250,000 persons who, according to Thomas G. Sherman, in his article on " The Owners of the United States," in the *Forum* of November, 1889, already possess this country. No one who knew that on one side of the Spring Valley case, there were a dozen and more of the greatest millionaires owning America, besides two or three very powerful and very impudent and very disloyal corporations, and that on the other side there were only a few thousand outraged citizens, would have dreamed that any governor would allow even a tone of sympathy for " the people " to escape him officially. It is safe in America for " rulers " to treat the people with contempt; it is not safe for them to thwart the plans of the money-power, not even if they are plans to rob and murder the poor. The money-power can prevent the nomination, election or confirmation of any official obnoxious to them. The people have no power in politics except to choose between two sets of candidates, selected by the mysterious forces of the caucus, and both wanting office only to do the work and get the boodle of the money-power. Why should a governor or his adjutant-general care for the people? They will beg for their votes like " Coriolanus " in Shakespeare's play, but only that, like Coriolanus, they may get the power with which to betray them and the republic.

CHAPTER X.

NOT content that these hapless people had been thus drawn into an ambush of starvation, and driven upon the wasting summit of a new and broader Starved Rock than that of the Indian legend which shadows the Illinois a few miles beyond Spring Valley, you have taken every means to rob them of the help and sympathy of the public. The siege was made one of moral as well as physical starvation. A stream of false information was poured into the ears of the country. Everything the miners said was garbled, all that they did misrepresented. To such an extent was this carried that it is literally true that not a single statement on any crucial point has been made by the company that was not misleading to the public and unjust to the men.

To alienate public sympathy, which was defeating the attempt to starve these men, your agents have dwelt with ceaseless iteration on the willingness of the men to live on charity instead of work, although almost all left their homes in search of work. You have stated repeatedly, as you did in your letter of August 24th, that you had offered the men $1.75 and $2 a day to work in your middle vein, and ingeniously made the unsophisticated public believe that your men refused it and preferred to live on charity rather than work. You omitted to state that your middle vein could give work to only fifty or one hundred men, only two or four out of every hundred you discharged, to all the rest of whom you refused all work. Nor did you state that the men offered to work there, but you would not listen to them because they came in committee. One of the latest instances of misrepresentation of the men was the statement in the letter to the citizens of Spring Valley, published November 1st, that " the final decision of the men is that they will not sign any contract nor be governed by any rules," the fact being that the men had made every effort to get a two-handled contract out of you, and had in mass-meeting agreed to abide by the rules of last year.

Very cunningly was the campaign of slander to check the streams of relief carried on. Only special knowledge of the subject could save

outsiders from being deceived, and this knowledge the public did not possess.   The pre-
possessions of many of the leaders of the business world were unalterably against the men,
and they willingly believed the evil report.
The essence of " business " is to get out of the
workingmen more than is given them.   It is
out of that margin of " profit " that our large
fortunes and gigantic business revenues are
scooped.   One of the great model merchants
of Chicago was asked for a contribution of
some of his canned beef tea, for the sick
women and children of Spring Valley.

" No," was the reply, " we will give nothing
to men on strike. "   His philosophy was clear
and simple.   The employer, like the king, can
do no wrong.   To explanations, assurances,
offers of proof that the trouble was not a strike,
but a lock-out, his ears were deaf.   The workingmen must be wrong.   But " nothing is
asked for the men," was then urged; this beef-
tea is wanted for the sick women and children,
and I promise you it shall be given only to
them, and only upon a physician's order."
Still deaf in heart and head.   " If the workingmen choose to place their wives and children
where they will die for want of food, or medicine, or doctors, so let it be.   We will not do

anything." Slanders against the miners lodged easily in such soil; to weed them out was hopeless. The inexperience of the general public made them ready dupes to the stories that the miners refused to work at high wages, because they wanted higher; that they were bad and desperate men; that the mines could not be operated in competition with the mines of southern Illinois unless wages were cut, etc. You assured the public, through your letter to the governor of September 25th, that there was no profit in the operation of the mines, and the public actually got to believe that your mines were a sort of eleemosynary entertainment run by you for the benefit of humanity in general, and your miners in particular, with no possibility of return to yourself. It now leaks out that, while making these statements to the public, a large stockholder in the coal company was buying up the interests of smaller holders. And while you were making these misstatements, other mines were working the same veins in your neighborhood with success. The White Breast Fuel Co. of Iowa, a powerful corporation, believed to be a sort of Siamese twin-brother of the Chicago, Burlington & Quincy Railroad, was spending a great many thousands of dollars at the same time a few miles away, in sinking shafts to reach the same veins.   Up to October all its shafts had been failures, owing to water or some other trouble, but the company cheerfully kept on sinking new shafts.   Its managers knew what they were about.   They had heard all about the bugaboo of " Southern Illinois competition."   They knew there was a prize in the Spring Valley neighborhood, and that it was well worth sinking thousands of dollars to get to it.   Such facts make it ridiculous to waste time over your assertion that the mines were not profitable.

Well informed, indeed, must he have been who could detect all the different varieties of untruths with which the cause of the men was met in street, parlor, newspaper, business office. During a visit at Spring Valley I learned at first hand that an offer had been made to the company, at the instigation of business men, anxious, naturally, to see the miners at work again, by about fifty miners, to work the middle vein, where only that number could then be employed.   The offer had been sent on to the head of the company for approval or the reverse.   Imagine the surprise with which I read in the next day's issue of one of the leading newspapers of the country a telegram

from Spring Valley announcing that the company had offered the miners this work, and that
the miners had refused it — just the reverse of
the facts.

In an interview with the manager of · the
company I asked why you had decreed the
destruction of the miners' union.

" Just look at that," he said, in a charmingly
confidential and I-don't-mind-telling-you-all-I-
know sort of air, " and you'll never ask that
question again."

What he had to show me was a little four-
page circular of the " By-Laws and Rules "
governing Lodge 26 of the Miners and Mine
Laborers.

" What is it you specially object to? " I
asked.

" All of it, but look particularly at this Rule
XIII.: ' Any man found with another man's
tools, shall be subjected to the following pen-
alties: First offense, suspension for ten working days; second offense, suspension for thirty
days; third offense, unconditional discharge
from the works.' Now," he said, " how would
you like to have your employés usurp the right
of discharging your workmen? "

Of course, I wouldn't like that if I were an
employer, and I said so. I went away con-

vinced that there was more in the " tyranny of labor organizations " than I had believed.

This was so important that I spent some time getting at the bottom of it.

The truth — carefully withheld by the manager — was, I found, that these dreadful rules and by-laws were a joint agreement which had been made between the company and the men for their mutual convenience in settling the various questions that arise in mining between employer and employé.   They were the company's rules as well as the men's.

The use of detectives has become a feature of the " harmony " between American labor and capital.   It is one of the most significant symptoms of the true condition of our industrial relations.   Espionage and tyranny have always gone together.   Power that has to uphold itself by the use of spies is, self-confessedly, a power that stands by force, not by consent.   The use of spies by a government shows that it is despotism, because it is not founded on the free consent of the governed. The use of spies by an employer is proof conclusive that the relations between him and his " hands " are not those of free contract.   It is one of the mischievous features of the present system that it has made the captains of industry so rich, and taken them so far away from actual touch with the people, that they have to depend on the report of intermediaries and detectives. These, by resistless laws of their kind of human nature, will tell their principals the things they think these would like to know, and will create, if they cannot discover, the conspiracies and bugaboos which make their services continuously indispensable. Spies sent from Pennsylvania worked in the Spring Valley mines for months before the lock-out of December, and it was no doubt largely on the report made by them that the policy of the company was determined. Detectives, claiming to be Pinkertons, were sent to town during the troubles between the company and the men. It was on the strength of the inebriated imagination of one of these worthless men that the idea gained credence · that the miners — the most peaceful men in the world — contemplated a resort to mob violence. These lying reports found ready echoes in the guilty consciousness of the company that its lock-out was a daily repeated act of violence against the lives of the people. The company's office was hastily converted into an arsenal, and repeating rifles with their deadly ammunition were sent in large quantities to

defend those whose only assailants were their
own consciences and the mercenary imagina-
tions of spies.   These detectives went so far
as to make their defiling rendezvous in the
church.

While the people, with incredible gentle-
ness, were bearing this great burden of want,
wondering, as Father Huntington said of them,
" with a look of bewilderment creeping over
their faces — wondering why they must die,"
your associated millions put out such assertions as this, over the signature of your representative, the president of the company,
in a letter in the Chicago *Times* of October
10th: " If property has depreciated in value, it
is the result of a condition of anarchy.   There
is no law in Spring Valley to-day.   Property
rights are not recognized there, nor is the life
of any man safe there, after dark unless it be
that of a man who is well armed and able to
protect himself."   This was indeed stoning
those who asked for bread.   Little need be
added to what Father Huntington says in his
letter on page 71, to show that these people
not only had not the brutal instincts which
could find gratification in violence, but had the
wit to know how irretrievably any disorder
would hurt them.   Such a slander could have

been uttered against this deeply injured community in this hour of suffering only by the
heart which had deliberately created misery to
make dividends.   It was not true, but it helped
create public opinion against the people, and
checked the relief.   The charge was especially
cruel, because Spring Valley has always been
phenomenally peaceful.   In four years there
has only been one murder there, and that was
done by a railroad hand, not a miner.   Crime
of all kinds has been practically unknown.
People went to bed safely without locking
their doors.   For a new town with a population of 5,000, gathered suddenly from all parts,
and out of all nationalities, this is a record
which can probably not be matched elsewhere.
It confirms what has been said about the select
character of the people.   They were the pick.

Even during the excited days when — no out-
break of any kind having taken place — the
streets were taken possession of by heavily
armed men, deputy sheriffs, called in because
the company said it expected trouble, and when,
following them, several companies of militia
came with loaded guns and fixed bayonets,
the people kept their temper on the whole
marvelously.   Some stones were thrown,
some windows broken.   The little disorder

there was, though not justifiable, was, Father Power declared, provoked by the behavior of the deputies. The grand jury of the county, mostly farmers, and not partial to labor unionists, could find nobody deserving of indictment, and when the militia went home, they sent back contributions for the relief of the people they had been summoned to shoot. Mr. Murtha, marshal of Spring Valley, says: " I have been a policeman in London and elsewhere in England, marshal in La Salle for many years, marshal here, I have been for twenty years in one way and another an officer of the peace, and in all that time I have never seen a quieter, more peaceful and law-abiding town than Spring Valley." This was said, too, during the lock-out, and after the affair of the deputy sheriffs, and the militia. The attitude of the miners when the deputy sheriffs and militia were quartered on the town suggests many resemblances to the behavior of the people of Boston under the provocations of the presence of the British soldiers in 1770, except that the miners were more patient than the Bostonians. The miners called the citizens to unite with them in a mass-meeting June 2d, at which the following preamble and resolutions were adopted:

WHEREAS, The Spring Valley Coal Company, after having locked us out since the 29th day of April, without having given us any information of why they did so; and,

WHEREAS, Having now brought to our city without cause or warrant the sheriff and posse, for the purpose of creating disturbance in our otherwise peaceable city, who have insulted and abused a number of our citizens who are pursuing their ways peaceably, not having violated any law; therefore, be it

Resolved, That we, the citizens of Spring Valley, condemn the action of the Spring Valley Coal Company as unwarranted, pernicious, and un-American, and calculated to disturb the peace of the city, thus prostituting the rights of our citizens to serve their private ends;

Resolved, That though these parties are here for the purpose of causing disturbance, we will thwart them in their efforts by counseling peace and a strict observance of the law, which they are determined to make us violate;

Resolved, That a committee be appointed to wait on Mayor Duggan and request him to assert his authority and bring to justice those parties who have been brought here without his leave or warrant.

We heard much from Spring Valley of another favorite accusation against the men: That they are prevented from working by their leaders, who are bad men, who terrorize the good men, etc.

In truth, every important step taken by the miners, as by labor unions generally, is by secret ballot.

The men vote just as they choose and in perfect security.

In this the labor organizations are far more democratic, far more observant of the opinions

and rights of dissentients than the organiza
tions of capital.   There is nothing in labor
unions comparable to the dictatorial power
exercised by the managers and trustees of
corporations.   The unionist has a freedom of
speech and vote on all questions, which the
stockholder does not know.

The miners were published to the world as
having " refused to accept their own offer," in
declining to work when the company in
October posted a notice calling for miners to
go into the middle vein at the wages which
the miners, through President McBride's letter,
had said would be satisfactory to them.   The
men were entirely right; they refused to go to
work because the company made it a necessary part of their proposal that the men should
give up their union, and make their contracts
as individuals.   To have surrendered this point
would have been to surrender something much
more important than the rate of wages.   They
did not " refuse their own offer," for the
recognition of their union was the most important part of their offer.   But this unjust
and untruthful color was given their action
and heralded through the country in press dis-
patches, and triumphantly quoted by the business class as another proof of the perfidious

and shiftless character of the working people. The ingenuity with which, in this and other countless ways, the course of these unfortunate miners has been tortured into seeming to be the opposite of what it really was, has been nothing short of diabolical.   Going among the men, nothing has interested me more than to see how this continuous and perverse misrepresentation of what they said and did mystified them, until in a kind of daze they came to accept it humbly, as part of their lot, something in the order of nature, that the well-to-do, the business class, should be forever unable or unwilling to understand them. Rather an unwise and unsafe attitude this, it has often seemed to me, for a minority, even if rich, to place themselves in with regard to the vast majority of the people.

It was the company, not the miners, which " refused to accept its own offer."   October 11th a notice was posted in the company's window, that a limited number of men were wanted to work in the middle vein, under " Streator rules and conditions."   It is part of the Streator rules that the men's organization is recognized by the company.

At a mass-meeting of the miners in Spring

Valley, October 11th, the following resolutions were passed:

Resolved, That we send a committee to Manager Dalzell to inform him that we will resume work on the same conditions as La Salle — namely, 82½ cents per ton and twenty inches of brushing.

Henry Hill, Joseph Hercer, and Archy Hamil were appointed on the above committee, with the addition of Messrs. W. Bailey, of the *Gazette*, and Mr. Johnson, of the *Sentinel.*

This committee retired from the meeting and had a short interview with Mr. Dalzell, who said he was instructed to have nothing to do with the committee in any manner, and he could not listen to any proposition from them, nor give them any satisfaction whatever.

The meeting had been called because of a notice being put up in the office window to the effect that the company was going to start the middle vein Monday, and would give employment to a limited number of men. The number of men that can be put to work in that vein is between 50 and 100. The committee asked Mr. Dalzell what the conditions in that vein would be. He told them he could not tell them as a committee; but, if any one applied for work as an individual, he would tell him. After much discussion, the miners arrived at the conclusion that the middle vein was being started for the same purpose as it was the 1st of June — to use fifty or sixty men for the purpose of enslaving several thousand — and that the purpose further was to break the miners' organization, which if accomplished would subject the miners to abuses they have before experienced, and with which the present reduction could not be compared. The following resolution was then adopted unanimously:

Resolved, That no man apply for work in the middle vein until the company is prepared to give all work and treat with us as a body.

In a communication to the press the miners explained that there are many men who cannot understand the English language, and, if they applied in person, they could not tell what conditions the company would impose in their contract. Of those who speak English there are many who would not properly understand the contracts, as the men claim that experience teaches that they are not couched in plain language, and that they need the closest investigation and consideration. The coal companies take every advantage of the miners when they succeed in compelling them to make agreements in this way; and then hold that they (the miners) are in honor bound to abide by them.

"All this trouble is being made by a few leaders who never dug a pound of coal," was another remark the representatives of the company often made to prejudice the public.

"Which of the leaders do you refer to?" I asked the superintendent, for all of them, as far as I knew, were practical miners, and had worked in the Spring Valley mines.

"There's Tom Brady, for one," he said; "he never swung a pick in his life."

"How is this, Brady?" I said to the secretary of the miners' organization, when I next saw him, "People say you have no right to represent the men, for you have never been a miner."

"Look at that scar," he said, rolling down his stocking; "that's where my leg was smashed by coal falling on it while I was working in the mines. I have never mined in Spring Valley, but I was check-weighman here, by the consent of both the men and the company, and the check-weighman must be a practical miner."

Even if the leaders were not miners, why should not the employed be as free to choose their representatives as the employer? The

president of the company never mined a ton
of coal.   The directors never mined a ton of
coal.   Are the rights of representative government in industry for the rich only?

This readiness to misrepresent any fact so
as to prevent the public from getting the materials for a true 'understanding of the case
went to recklessness and beyond.   Turning
back to the advertisements offering lots for
sale on pages 24 and 29, the reader will see that
they are all signed by the Spring Valley Coal
Company.   These advertisements were circulated in newspapers and pamphlets for five years;
hundreds of thousands of dollars' worth of lots
were sold through them, and yet the president
of the coal company, who has acted as your
spokesman throughout the whole business, declared to the public, over his own signature, in
a letter dated October 8th, in the Chicago
Times: " The Spring Valley Coal Company
has never, so far as my knowledge goes, offered lots for sale.   It has never, to my knowledge, disposed of any of its realty.   The sale
and purchase of lots at Spring Valley have
been entirely private transactions with which
the company has had nothing to do."   If the
reader will compare these amazing assertions
with the closing lines of the advertisements

given above on pages 24 and 29, he will fit himself to judge correctly of the value of all the other assertions coming from your representatives.

One of the officers of the company repeated to me the favorite refrain of their letters, interviews, and statements that the men did not want to go to work, and had made no effort to get back to work.

I knew better than that, and said: " It is only a few days since the men decided, in their mass-meeting, to make you an offer to go to work in your middle vein, at the same prices paid in Streator, where about fifty could be employed, and sent you a committee with the proposition."

" We don't recognize committees," was the reply.

Because the men had come in a committee, this gentleman was willing to make the statement that " the men " had never tried to get work.

To any one of the general public too little familiar with the facts to detect the lurking lie, this assertion would have conveyed the impression it was made to convey, that the company was anxious to open the mines, and that the men didn't want work, and would rather live on charity.

11

The public has been misled by your agents about the facts of the business, as well as about the doings of the workingmen.   In their various communications to the public the coal company have dwelt, as the main line of defense, and with great effect, on the competition of the coal of southern Illinois.   They have succeeded thereby in creating the widespread belief that this cheaper southern coal was driving the dearer coal of Spring Valley, and the rest of northern Illinois, out of the market.   Speaking of this, the president of the company says: " The operators in northern Illinois cannot pay from 30 to 50 per cent. more for mining their coal and compete in the markets with coal costing from 30 to 50 per cent. less for mining."   Again, he says: " If we could mine and produce our coal at Spring Valley at the same cost that it is mined and produced for in southern Illinois we would then be on an equal footing in these markets," etc.

By these, and many other reiterations of the same point, the idea was thoroughly disseminated among the public to the disadvantage of the miners, that they persisted in demanding wages at which the northern Illinois mines were being driven out of business by the southern Illinois mines.   This was done so successfully that the first point made against the writer whenever I began a discussion with a business acquaintance, of the case of the Spring Valley miners, was sure to be: " It is impossible for these mines, with their thin veins, to compete with the thick veins of the southern mines.   If the miners won't take less the Spring Valley Coal Company says it will have to shut its mines for good."

Fortunately, or unfortunately, according to the point of view, the facts of this bugbear competition of southern with northern Illinois coal are accessible to all.   They disclose that it is a phantom, a shadow good enough to fight the claims of the working people with, but not good enough to stand the light of investigation.   This would be more than surprising if we had not had in this whole degrading business so many other illustrations of the same mongering of facts.   In truth, the trade morality of our day thinks it all right for one bargainer to mislead another as far as he can. " Let the buyer beware."   Special Commissioners Gould and Wines made a thorough inquiry into the excuse thus proffered for the terrible course taken at Spring Valley, and report that there is nothing in it.   Nothing in it ! The whole fabric of the company's justification of its action in inaugurating the lock-out, in the application of the hunger-screw to get lower wages, rests on the allegation that they were made necessary by this southern competition. The president of the Spring Valley Company said, in his letter to Governor Fifer, September 25th, justifying the offer of 35 cents a ton : " We have made all the concessions that we can possibly make to our men and be able to maintain ourselves in a competitive market. "

But the special commissioners of the State of Illinois report, officially, that there is nothing in it. This ground of defense occupies the principal place in all the company's statements. The facts will be found given in full on pages 13 and 14 of Messrs. Gould and Wines' report. Their conclusions are thus stated :

" In 1883 the first mining district and Bureau County,* taken together, reported 25.6 per cent. of the total output of the State, and 27 per cent. of the value of all the coal produced; while in 1888 they reported 30 per cent. of the total output of the State, and 36.4 per cent. of the value of all the coal pro-

---

* Spring Valley is in Bureau County.

duced.   They had gained on their rivals, within the State, in five years, 4.4 per cent. in tonnage, and 9.4 per cent. in price, instead of losing ground, as they claim that they have been doing for a long series of years past." *

The commissioners conclude: " We dismiss from further consideration by us the claim that the diminution of profits in mining in the first and second districts is due to the increased production of coal in southern Illinois.   It appears to us to be not only not proved, but disproved by such statistics as are at our command."

A deep condemnation is pronounced upon you in these colorless official words.

Your lock-out was unnecessary.

Your nicely built defense, with facts and figures so skillfully dovetailed, is a sham.

What aspect does this put upon your treatment of these people?

The contradictions and absurdities in the statements put out by these great business geniuses, speak for themselves.   For instance:

Your spokesman figured out in his letter of August 24th, that, if the miners' demand of 85 cents a ton were conceded, the company would

---

* On account of the lock-out no comparison can be made with the figures of 1889.

lose 17½ cents a ton.   It was then offering 35, nominally 75, cents a ton for mining.   It has since settled at 82½ cents, 2½ cents less than the figure on which the above calculation of loss was estimated.   If these figures were correct, it is now losing about 15 cents a ton.   It was to get the opportunity of losing 15 cents a ton that the manager of the company based the offer of his superintendent to take the mines and pay him a bonus of 15 cents a ton.   It was for the privilege of losing 15 cents a ton that he has been printing and scattering broadcast pamphlets, "To Miners," urging them to go to Spring Valley, has been appealing almost with frenzy to the public for their support through every channel possible, has more than doubled his first offer to the men.   It is by doing business on this principle of losing 15 cents a ton, no doubt, that the enormous fortunes represented in the Spring Valley enterprise have been created.

Is it not strange that, of such transparent juggling as this with common sense and business sense, public opinion should be made?

These incidents give only a glimpse into the methods of this campaign of slander and siege, of moral starvation.

Where will public indignation find the words

to express itself when it realizes that the purpose of these misrepresentations was to cut off
the sympathy of the world from these poor and
betrayed men, so that, unrelieved, they might
be forced by your partners, hunger and cold,
to sell you their lives below cost?

CHAPTER XI.

FEED MY LAMBS.

THE men who went to work, in November, after the surrender, got no pay from the company until the middle of December. They got credit at the stores, but there were many families whose heads were away, many who could not get work, because the mines are not yet cl:ared up, and therefore could not get credit. The distress of the summer, therefore, continued into midwinter. This was anticipated by Adjutant-General Vance in his report given above, in which he says that the necessity for relief would probably exist for several weeks after the mines have resumed operations.

November 27th one of the leading men among the miners wrote in a private letter: " A great many of our men have not started to work yet, as only a limited number can possibly work at the repairing.   *   *   *   There are some who have a hard time to keep body and soul together. We have no money in the

(168)

treasury. The men are in a poor condition, and somewhat discouraged."

An inquiry was consequently sent to a resident of Spring Valley, asking what relief was still needed, and to whom it should be sent. His reply puts the last touch to this picture of man's inhumanity to man. With other information, it was the basis of the following dispatch, furnished by the writer and sent out by the Associated Press on Thanksgiving Day, 1889:

CHICAGO, November 28.—The Spring Valley Coal Company, to prepare people to celebrate Thanksgiving, have refused employment upon re-opening the mines to miners who, during the lock-out just ended, took a leading part in the distribution of food, clothing and medicine to the sick and starving. This relief forced the company to make terms twice as good as those offered, although it did not save the men from severe reduction. The company has also declined to re-employ officers of labor unions, and has compelled all miners to abandon unions. As there is no other industry in Spring Valley except that of this coal company, this refusal to employ banishes the members of the relief committee and leaders of the union from Spring Valley. They are penniless, having had no work for seven months, like all the working people here.

Some of these banished men have families of seven and eight children. This action of the company has so intimidated the other miners that they decline receiving contributions for those still in want. They are afraid that if they are found distributing relief they will be also told to leave. Distress will last at least until midwinter, as the mines are ready for only a few men, and the heads of many families are away looking for work. November earnings will be small, and not paid until the middle of December. Relief will be needed, but the union has been broken up, and the miners do not dare form another relief committee.

Here was a speedy illustration of what the surrender of the union meant to the men when worn out by the ceaselessly applied torture of famine, they went back to work as "individuals." When Mr. Bourke, who had been president of the union, applied for work along with the rest who had stampeded, he was told that there was no place for him. When Mr. McNulty, who had been secretary, made a similar application, he got a similar answer. Henry Hill, too, has had to go. He was never an officer of the union, never took any lead in any dispute with the company. He has been banished because, when the women and children and the men who could not get work began to starve, he gave himself to the duty of relief. He was made chairman of the relief committee. He worked day and night dividing the provisions that were given, scouring the country for more, hunting out the worst cases of distress. He fed your hungry, he bound up your wounded, he visited your sick. As he did it to these; he did it unto Him whom you call Lord! Lord! and, for doing it, you have said to him, " Move on. There is no place for you in Spring Valley with your seven

children and your wife. Take to the road.
You tried to save the lives we were trying to
cheapen." C. W., too, whose story I have told
above, when he applied for work, after the surrender, got the word which meant, " Move on.
You shall not live in Spring Valley if we can help
it." He was never an officer of the union,
never represented the men in any of their differences with the company, has always worked
faithfully according to his bargain. His only
offense was that he had been a member of the
relief committee, and that he had fed " Him
who was a hungered," who, as " Chinese
Gordon " says, lives to-day in the persons of
the poor and suffering.

These men and the others refused work
were sober, industrious, good men. The
" sacred right to work," of which we hear so
much, was denied them, simply because they
had been chosen by their associates to act for
them in the union or the relief work, and had
done it to the best of their ability. The refusal of work is, so far as the coal company
had control, the refusal of the privilege of
living at Spring Valley, since there is no other
industry there, as the advertisements stated,
except coal mining, and the coal is all owned
by you of the coal company. Some of the

blacklisted men got public work to do for the
city ; the others have gone.   The men who
have acted, as you would say of your own representatives, as " attorneys," or " directors,"
or " purchasing agents," or " brokers," or
what not, for their fellows, as yours worked
for you in this very matter, have been for that
offense banished with their families.   To get
lower and lower wages, and more and more
work out of your men, it is indispensable that
they should not be allowed to unite, that they
should be starved, that, when starved, they
should be cut off from outside relief, and that
any natural leaders who show themselves
should be weeded out.   So these men must
move on, like Poor Joe, although they had no
money to move with, no place to go to, and
winter was on them.   If they had bought lots,
not fully paid for, they must forfeit land and
money.   Christian warfare stops murdering its
enemies when they pull down their flag ; but
business and the Apaches take a surrender
only to facilitate extermination.

The men had anticipated the possibility of
such tactics, and had endeavored to guard
against them.   Before surrendering, knowing
it to be the practice of employers to black-
list the leaders of the men during strike or

lock-out, the miners put to the president of the company, the direct question, whether, if the men went back to work, he would agree that the leaders should also be employed. They received in reply the following explicit assurance over his own signature: " Regarding those men who may be considered the leaders, and who are so largely responsible for our difficulties, but who have not been parties to any overt acts toward the company, we will make no exceptions to their returning to work and remaining in the employ of the company, so long as they in good faith live up to what they agree to do. We have arranged to send men to Spring Valley, and we are meeting with more success than we expected."

Badly whipped as they were, the men were too honorable to go back to work, and leave their leaders to be sacrificed. They would have continued the hopeless fight still longer, rather than submit to that. But this declaration from the president of the company was explicit and satisfactory. It came from a foe, but still from a foe they supposed to be an honorable one.

Immediately upon receiving this assurance, that their leaders would not be discriminated against, the men voted to go back to work. Then they found that the pledge had been given only to lure them to surrender. In its public card in the following pages, it will be seen, the company does not venture to make any pretense that the banished men had been guilty of any offense. If a tale of such duplicity were put into a novel on the labor question, all the critics would cry out against such inartistic, because impossible, fiction.

Neither State nor nation has the power by law to banish, but America's millionaires claim and exercise it, though it is a function which the government itself would not dare to assert.

The feeling with which this news was received by the country was expressed with eloquent indignation by the New York *Herald* in the following editorial, in its issue of November 29th:

A DISGRACE TO CIVILIZATION.

It is almost incredible that the Spring Valley Coal Company should upon reopening its mines refuse employment to the miners who took food, clothing and medicine to sick and hungry folks during the terrible lock-out, and yet such is the news telegraphed from Chicago yesterday.

A more brutal and damnable action can hardly be conceived in a civilized community. It has cowed the relief committees, and supplies have ceased. Disease and starvation may stalk unchecked among the helpless women and children.

When spring comes the sleek directors of this wealthy corporation can point to the graves of those who perish this winter, and say to their slaves: "If you would save your dear ones from this fate, take the wages we offer you without murmuring." Then the directors may go back to their homes and thank God that they live in a land of liberty and charity.

The president of the company replied to the statements made in the Associated Press dispatch by issuing a card, which, on account of its gross and angry personalities, the Associated Press declined to circulate. Omitting the " abuse of the plaintiff's attorney," the card said:

There has been no order given to not employ men at Spring Valley who took "a leading part in the distribution of food during the strike," as is alleged, nor as to any miner who was engaged in the strike. When the men accepted the company's terms, which were more liberal as to the price of mining than the price paid at other mines in the State, more men signed contracts the first day than we could possibly put to work, and miners have been leaving other mines in the State and flocking to Spring Valley in such numbers since work was resumed that it has been impossible for the company to find work for all of them.

Owing to the long strike our mines were not in condition to work at their full capacity when work was resumed. We are doing all we can, night and day, to get them in order, which we hope to do by the middle of December, when we will be in shape to double, if not treble, the number of men we are now working. No better refutation of the infamous slanders and misrepresentations heaped upon the Spring Valley Coal Company and its officers can be given than the fact that not only have all of our old men signed contracts, but that miners are coming to Spring Valley from all over the State, seeking work without our solicitation. Men generally go where they are best paid, and where they can earn the most money.

In reply to the *Herald*, the president of the company wrote a card, in the course of which he said:

I do not ask or expect the public or press of the country to accept any statements made by my company in refutation of the misrepresentation and falsehoods that a partisan press has subjected the Spring Valley Coal Company and its officers to during the past six months, but I do claim that official statements and records made by the authorities of the State of Illinois ought to be accepted by a fair and impartial press as a refutation of these slanders. Governor Fifer, of Illinois, a republican, through his adjutant-general and the State Board of Charities, during the past summer, and when the strike of the miners had been on from four to six months, made a thorough investigation of the condition of affairs at Spring Valley, and the official report of these gentlemen is the best answer that I can give to the infamous slanders and misrepresentations which have been published in the press of the country.

Why there should be any suffering or destitution at Spring Valley on Thanksgiving, when a miner can earn from $3 to $5 per day for the support of himself and his family, I am unable to account for.

The following extract accompanied the letter, though, as the reader will see, it has nothing whatever to do with the subject of the *Herald's* editorial.

My inquiries were more particularly made with a view to ascertain the conditions as to the destitution, starvation, suffering, sickness and general sanitary condition. I requested the mayor to point out the most prominent cases of destitution or to have the supervisor of the township, who is ex-officio overseer of the poor, do so, as I would prefer to base my representation of the situation to you upon personal observation. The citizens with whom I conversed were representatives of the population of Spring Valley, and included physicians, druggists, police, butchers, mechanics, miners, merchants, professional men and business men generally.

The general sentiment expressed by these persons was that the memorial presented to you and signed by many of them was a misrepresentation as to the condition in reference to destitution, starvation, suffering and sickness; that without any consultation or concert of action on their part, the memorial was prepared and submitted to them for signature. Some persons said they were opposed to the memorial as a whole; that no such condition existed as was represented; that there was no starvation, destitution or sickness worthy of mention, but that they had signed the memorial because, if they refused to do so, they would be boycotted in business. Others seemed to take a different view. While they freely admitted the exaggeration in reference to starvation and destitution, yet they urged that there had been a necessity for charitable work, and that this necessity would probably exist for several weeks after the miners had resumed operations.—*Extract from James W. Vance's Report.*

Concerning the card in the New York *Times*, the Philadelphia *Press* said:

The facts in this case are clear. The president of the coal company and his associates made money in the Spring Valley mines by methods which led to a strike by starving men. These methods were exposed by that well-known Episcopal clergyman, Father Huntington, and by others. The exposure aroused public sympathy and led to public aid, which rendered the strike successful. There is even reason to believe that it will advance wages throughout the Illinois mines. Replying to published letters asserting that the company was refusing work to miners engaged in relief distribution, to officers in the union and to all who would not leave the union, the president of the company denies that "orders" to this effect were issued, and asserts that "all our old men have signed contracts." We

sincerely hope this is true. We would like to believe that even
he has seen the error of his ways. We hope he has. At the
same time, a more direct denial would have been better adapted
to convince, and he could clinch it by a brief statement from
the union or its officers.

To the cards in the *Times* and *Herald*, the
following rejoinder was made. It was circulated by the Associated Press, and, as the
comments of a large number of papers showed,
was universally accepted as the indisputable
truth of the matter :

The Spring Valley Coal Company denies the truth of the
statement sent out by the Associated Press, that the coal company refused employment, upon reopening the mines, to the
miners who took a leading part in the distribution of food,
clothing and medicine to the sick and starving, and to the officers of the union during the lock-out, and has also compelled
the miners to give up their union. The statement was true ;
the denial is untrue. It is vital the fact should be understood,
not to make or unmake any one's reputation for veracity, but
that the public may know what means are being employed to
terrorize and impoverish the working people.

In a letter written the day before Thanksgiving a prominent
member of the Spring Valley Relief Committee said :

" The company are putting the men to work as fast as they
can—that is, the men they want to give work to. Seven of us
have been refused work, and five of those seven for certain will
get no work in Spring Valley. Their names are James O'Hare,
Andrew Bourke, Thomas McNulty, Chris Weimer and Henry
Hill. They will have to go and seek work elsewhere, which is
pretty 'hard law' in the winter, after seven months' idle time.
As far as sending relief here now is concerned, none of the
miners would take anything to distribute for fear they would be
dealt with like these five, and be made victims and have to leave

the place. If you could do anything to find work for me I would go to Chicago."

Confirmation of these statements is right at hand from the other side. In its issue of Thanksgiving Day the Spring Valley *Gazette*, the organ of the business men, not the workingmen, said :

"At the miners' meeting Monday evening the men donated $118 to help out of town a few men who have not yet got work from the coal company. Six men are on the list—namely: A. D. Bourke, Harry Hill, Thomas McNulty, Clement Lalliment, Ed. Travis, and Chris Weimer. The $118 was the entire balance of the money remaining in the hands of the relief committee."

Of these men who are "on the list," Bourke was the president and McNulty the secretary of the Miners' Union up to the end of the lock-out, Hill was the chairman of the Relief Committee, and the others active members.

A later letter states that four of the men, Bourke, Hill, Lalliment, and McNulty, the leaders of the union and the Relief Committee, have gone into their involuntary exile, and by the same mail comes the Spring Valley *Gazette* stating that Bourke has gone as far away as Missouri. These men have to leave their wives and children behind them.

As to the union the miners, besides submitting to the banishment of their old leaders, are compelled to sign contracts by which they bind themselves, individually, not to take part in any combination to obtain better wages, and agree to leave the settlement of all grievances to the sole judgment and decision of the company. The company refuses the union any recognition in matters between itself and the men.

The value of the company's denial may be sufficiently judged from the fact that the only quotation it makes from the Associated Press dispatch is garbled by changing the word lock-out to strike. The trouble at Spring Valley was officially declared to be not a strike but a lock-out by the special commissioners employed by the governor of Illinois to investigate it. The anxiety of the company to mislead the public on this point is evidence that they cannot afford to stand by their action in applying the torture of famine for seven months to 5,000 people in order to buy their labor " below cost."

The New York *Sun* of December 16, 1889, in printing this statement, said, editorially: "It is a conclusive reply."

The Philadelphia *Press* said: " Denials count for little in the face of these facts, and, if the president of the coal company wants any one to believe him, he must meet these painstaking and accurate statements not with abuse, but with proof that his company has given work to the men whose only crime was distributing charity to their mates."

And the Pittsburg *Dispatch* declared that this recapitulation of the facts made "fine mince-meat" of the denial by the company.

No further denial was attempted. Any one who has made himself familiar with the facts of this case, and has a taste for the work, can pick out dozens of contradictions and obvious misstatements in the statements made by the company. But it is a profitless task to spend time hunting for dropped stitches in a web, the warp and woof of which are spun altogether out of deceit and wrong-doing. But it is worth while, in passing, to point out a characteristic illustration of the reckless will-

ingness of these employers to make a point
regardless of the facts. In its card of November 29th, the company stated that it " has
been impossible for the company to find work
for all of them " — the miners who had applied
for employment. But the next day, in the
card of November 30th, the spokesman of
the company says:

" Why there should be any suffering or destitution at Spring Valley on Thanksgiving,
when a miner can earn from $3 to $5 a day
for the support of himself and his family, I am
unable to account for."

Friday the needs of self-defense created a
demand for some such statement as that the
company had not refused employment, but
had been unable to give it to all. That statement was supplied accordingly. Saturday
created a demand for the statement that the
company had furnished all with employment
yielding $3 to $5 a day, and that statement
was supplied forthwith.

Such are the advantages of life-long practice
of the principles of supply and demand.

But the company, in their first denial, make
one assertion, upon which it will be profitable
to pause. Your spokesman says:

" No better refutation of the infamous slan-

ders and misrepresentations heaped upon the
Spring Valley Coal Company and its officers
can be given than that not only have all of our
old men signed contracts, but that miners
are coming to Spring Valley from all over
the State seeking work without our solicitation."

The writer of the card conceived, as he wrote
that, to say "All of our old men have signed
contracts" would sound well, and he said it,
utterly untrue as it was, as the facts we have
given show. But that is a mere aside, which
can be dismissed as an extemporaneous caper
in a life-long waltz with fancy. But the closing declaration that the miners who had flocked
into Spring Valley, upon the resumption of
work, had come there "without solicitation,"
conceals a maneuver so deliberate, so characteristic of this whole business, and so mischievous, that it must not be passed by.

In the Spring Valley *Gazette* of November
14, 1889, when the company was in the thick
of the negotiations with its locked-out men for
their return to work, this paragraph was
printed:

" ' A Word to Miners' is the title of a neat
eight-page pamphlet received Monday from
Erie, Pa. It is descriptive of the city of Spring

Valley, and the mines to which it refers, in glowing terms."

Erie, Pa., is the home of the president and spokesman of the coal company. The pamphlet is herewith given in full. It is an important document.

A WORD

TO

COAL MINERS.

A WORD TO COAL MINERS.

There is no State in the Union containing a larger Bituminous Coal area in proportion to its square miles than the State of Illinois, and there are no mines in the United States where a miner can have steadier work at more remunerative wages than can be had at the most favorably located mines in northern Illinois. There is a reason for this that can be readily understood by any intelligent miner: In the first place the consumption of Bituminous Coal for steam purposes, by railroads, is enormous in that section, arising from the fact that Illinois contains more miles of completed railroad to its population than any other State in the Union. The consumption of coal by these railroads is a steady one throughout the year, which is a great advantage in the way of furnishing steady work to the wageworker. The northern boundary of the coal fields of the State, where the veins of coal are well defined and regular in their formation, terminates at about the 41st parallel of latitude, at a point where the Illinois River reaches its most northern limit. The great States of Wisconsin and Minnesota, as well as portions of Illinois and Michigan north of the 42d parallel, are destitute of coal. The coal from these northern Illinois fields also finds a ready market in the States and Territories west and northwest of the State of Illinois. With fully seven months of winter and the thermometer often falling to 30 or 40 degrees below zero throughout this large area, with its large and active population, practically without timber, coal is not only a necessity in the great cities, but also to the farming community. By referring to the geological map of the State of Illinois, it will be seen that the northern limit of the coal fields of the State, as stated, is between the 41st and 42d parallels of latitude, and it will also be observed that the great city of Chicago is within the same parallels.   Drawing a line due east and west through Chicago, and north and south through Spring Valley, Illinois, it will be found that the Spring Valley mines are about 55 miles south of the east and west line, and about 100 miles west of Chicago, midway between the waters of the great lakes and the Mississippi River, and that the great lower and upper veins of the Illinois fields do not extend beyond eight miles north of Spring Valley, and that their southern terminus is in the 37th parallel of latitude, being about the southern boundary of the State. This great middle field, as officially laid down by the geological map of the State of Illinois, cannot be better described than by comparing it with a ham, the huck starting at Spring Valley, Illinois, and extending south.   Within this formation, only the middle or upper veins are found.   East and west of it, to a greater or lesser extent, the great underlying veins are found, but in no instance are the upper and lower veins found together in their complete formation outside of the counties of La Salle and Bureau, and even in these two counties not exceeding 40,000 to 50,000 acres.   Taking Chicago as the great railroad center of the West, with its present population of over 800,000 people, and its prospective growth, it is hard to even approximate what its future coal consumption will be.   We know that in 1888 Chicago consumed over three millions of tons of Bituminous Coal, and it is within bounds to say that the railroad consumption of coal by the roads extending north, west, and southwest of Chicago, for steam purposes, during the same period, was not less than five millions of tons.   If you want to sell coal, or in fact any other commodity, you must find a market for it.   A large market means a large consumption, and a large consumption means steady work for the producers of the commodity consumed, as well as fair wages for the wage-worker; and, if there are any coal fields in the United States better located in this respect than the mines at Spring Valley, we have yet to find them.

When the last geological map of the State of Illinois was issued in 1875, the fact was not then known that the Spring

Valley coal fields contained both the middle and lower veins of coal of the State; but practical working has fully demonstrated this fact. There are three well defined and workable veins of coal at Spring Valley, the first vein averaging about four feet, and, at a depth of 150 feet, has not been worked. The second vein is from five to seven feet thick, at a depth of 250 feet below the surface, with a good roof and comparatively free from water, and is worked on the room and pillar system.

A good miner doing an honest day's work, can mine from four to five tons per day, and are now doing it, which at the present price paid for mining in that vein, namely, 72½ cents per ton, will enable him to earn from $3.25 to $4 per day, and the men now working are making these wages. The lower vein, 350 feet below the surface, is mined on the long wall system. The coal is from three feet eight inches to four feet thick. The under-cutting is mainly in fire clay, although in some of the rooms or faces in two of the shafts, the rock is found underlying the coal to a limited extent in some of the working places. The roof is soapstone, about fourteen feet thick, and about twenty-four inches of it above the coal has to be removed. There is no water in the lower vein; it is practically free from faults; the level of the vein will not vary five feet in a mile; no powder is required; after the bearing in is done, the coal falls from the compression of the roof. Two men are allowed a face of forty-two feet to work in. The percentage of the nut and slack combined is only thirteen per cent. The screens are seven-eighths of an inch, and the price paid for mining this vein is 82½ cents per ton of 2,000 pounds of screened coal, including twenty-four inches of brushing. A good miner can mine four tons per day, and in many cases five tons.

THE TOWN OF SPRING VALLEY.

Less than four years ago, where the town of Spring Valley now stands, was an open prairie containing a few scattered farm houses. The town is located at a bend on the northern bluff of the Illinois River, from 90 to 100 feet above same, in the counties of Bureau and La Salle, on a high rolling prairie. No more beautiful, fertile, and productive agricultural region can be found on this continent than is tributary to Spring Valley. In less than one year from the time work began in developing the mines, there were 1,000 inhabitants in the town, and in 1888 the population was estimated to be between 4,500 and 5,000 people. Fine brick blocks, churches, schools, private residences, hotels, national bank, electric lights, water supply, and last but not least, snug and comfortable houses for the wage-worker, were constructed as if by magic. Three trunk lines of railroad pass through Spring Valley, two of which have been extended there since the town was started, namely, the Chicago, Burlington & Quincy, and the Chicago & North-Western, the Chicago, Rock Island & Pacific being the third. No town of its size and certainly no coal property has superior railroad and shipping facilities than Spring Valley, and in addition, by the Illinois River, it possesses an uninterrupted water communication with the Gulf of Mexico. The development of the Spring Valley Company's property and the output of coal reached in so short a period, has been phenomenal, and as the main product is produced under the long wall system, being the largest mines worked under this system in the United States, if not in the world, to-day, its ability to meet all possible demands upon it in the future, is equal to that of any Bituminous Coal mines in the country. There are six shafts or mines now open, and when fully developed and in operation, will have a capacity of not less than 1,000 tons of coal per day each; in 1888 the output per day reached as high as 4,000 tons. To the steady, sober and industrious coal miner, no better locality can be found to locate in than Spring Valley, and no coal field where steadier work and the highest wages paid for mining coal can be relied upon. To the industrious miner willing to do a fair day's work for a fair day's wage, and who wishes to own his own home, and live " under his own vine and fig tree," the Spring Valley Company are prepared to erect such homes for them, to be paid for in monthly installments, on long time, at a rate of interest not exceeding five per cent. per annum on the actual cost of the house and lot, and these monthly installments will be so little in excess of the rent usually paid for such premises, that at the end of a few years the wage-worker will have his own home. The Spring Valley Coal Company do not want agitators, bummers or drunkards, nor will they employ such knowingly. Men who live off of the labor of others and whose occupation is dependent upon their ability to excite strikes and differences between the wage-worker and the operator, are the worst enemies of labor. Every intelligent employer of labor should know that his interests can be best promoted by paying the . highest possible wages his business will permit, and by making those who work for him feel that he has an interest in their prosperity and welfare, and that he is ready and willing at all times to concede to the individual wage-worker his just and equitable rights.

HOW TO GET TO SPRING VALLEY.

It takes two or three hours to reach Spring Valley from Chicago by the Chicago, Rock Island & Pacific Railroad, and the fare is $3. The Spring Valley Coal Company can now give steady work to additional miners, with good tenement or boarding houses to live in, at reasonable prices. Men who are accustomed to mining anthracite coal, iron ore, or other minerals, can soon successfully work at Spring Valley.

Those desiring further information, can address:

Genl. Manager, Spring Valley, Ill.

Genl. Agent, Chicago, Ill.

SPRING VALLEY, ILL., November 1st, 1889.

This pamphlet re-enforces the exhibition made by the advertisements and pamphlets described above and used to " boom " the town. It shows how systematic and expensive were the solicitations to new miners to come to Spring Valley, to buy lots, to overstock the labor market, and to menace the locked-out men already there with the permanent loss of their places. It baits again the old trap of the "home" and "the vine and fig tree." It is silent as the sphinx about your lock-out, still in force, which had lasted eleven months for one-third the men and seven months for all of them, ignoring that, it renews the promises, so cruelly falsified, of the original rainbow advertisements of " steady work" and the "highest wages.", The terms in which it describes the six shafts " now open," and the price which " is " paid of 82½ cents a ton, are obviously designed to conceal the fact that no wages were being earned at all, and that the six shafts were closed to all the men, except fifty or sixty who were working in the middle vein. The uninformed miner reading this pamphlet would believe Spring Valley to be in the mid-career of busy prosperity; not until he arrived would he learn the truth, and discover that the invitation he had accepted was but a " busi-

ness man's" maneuver to use him against
brother workingmen. This pamphlet was
openly addressed to miners. It was dated
November 1st, it was widely circulated, it is
signed by the officers of the company, it soli-
cits miners to come to Spring Valley, even
gives the railroad fare from Chicago; and yet
the spokesman of the company has the face to
declare, in a public card over his own signature four weeks later, that the miners who
filled Spring Valley came there "without our
solicitation."

When the president of the Spring Valley
Coal Company says the miners now in Spring
Valley came "without solicitation," he has
to face even more damnatory evidence than
this pamphlet. In his letter of November 2d,
to the men quoted above on page 171, he says:
"We have arranged to send men to Spring
Valley, and are meeting with more success than
we expected."

It is by such strokes of "enterprise" that
the conditions of dissatisfaction and the sense
of wrong are created among the working
people.

It is seldom that facts like these — as real
facts of supply and demand as any others —
get to the public. Professors of political

13

economy do not come near enough to realities to discover these things; the workingmen do not know how to bring them before public opinion. All possible pains are taken to conceal these tactics, to keep them subterranean, and deny them, as is done in this case. But it is such deceit and betrayal and false guidance that make the difference to the workingman between mere subsistence and killing poverty. To the employer they mean success in getting lower wages and higher dividends; he lives at the comfortable altitude where the alternations of the economic climate are only between the more and less of too much. He seems to be unable to understand the suffering or the resentment of the working people whom his business stratagems (so pleasant to him) reduce from too little to nothing.

CHAPTER XII.

" MILLIONS IN IT! "

" How can such things be true? " the public ask, appalled. " Even if there is no humanity or justice in these men, their interest ought to restrain them. They lose when their mines are shut, the sales of land arrested, the company store closed, the coal traffic of the North-Western suspended. What can the motive be? These men are not monsters who would torture the poor when there is no money in it for them."

There is money in it. There is millions in it.

It has been a good speculation for all of you, this successful attempt to cheapen the men and destroy their union. Besides the profit that will be made by forfeiting all the money,* and regaining possession of the lands

---

* The latest news from Spring Valley is that the company is pushing the men hard for back payments on the lots bought by them previous to the lock-out. In almost all cases this must end in the forfeiture of the lot and all the money so far paid in. This forfeiture will be the direct result of the lock-out, and the company will make a handsome profit out of its own wrongdoing — thereby violating one of the fundamental principles on which social life is based.

of those who cannot finish paying for them,
there has been secured a reduction of wages,
which will of itself roll up, in the course of
years, to thousands per cent. of profit on the
whole investment. The coal company has
40,000 acres of coal land, or sixty-six square
miles, the largest estate of any coal-mining
company in the world.

The circular, " A Word to Miners," quoted
above, states that there are " three well-defined
and workable veins, the first at a depth of 150
feet, averaging four feet   *   *   *
the second, 250 feet below the surface, five to
seven feet thick.   *   *   *   the
third, 350 feet below the surface, three feet
eight inches to four feet thick." The formula
used by mining engineers in these fields to find
the amount of coal in these veins gives 1,000
tons of coal per acre to every foot of thickness
in the vein. Hence according to the company's statement that its three veins foot up
about fourteen feet thick it must have 14,000
tons of coal per acre for the whole 42,000
acres This would be 560,000,000 tons in all
On the cost of digging this, they have secured
by their war on the striking men a reduction
of not less than ten cents a ton, besides advantages in the iron-clad contract worth added

money. This saving of ten cents a ton on your 560,000,000 tons makes the pretty penny of $56,000,000. The total investment of the coal company has not been much more than $1,000,000 — it pays taxes on only $166,994 — and this single campaign, according to its own figures of the amount of coal, yields a profit of 5,000 per cent. and more; a profit from this single summer's campaign of over $50 for every dollar invested.

You have no right to growl with these figures, for they are your own. But the truth is they are incorrect. The company, in its " Word to Miners," grossly exaggerated the amount of coal to be mined, and did so as a part of its tactics to beguile innocent and trusting workingmen into its paradise of " steady employment " " at $3.50 to $4 a day." But the public must not be misinformed, even though it would serve the company right to let its figures stand to its own confusion. Mining engineers who have made a thorough investigation of the coal fields in the vicinity of Spring Valley agree that there are, as nearly as can be figured out, about 5,000 tons per acre. On this basis, your mines will yield 200,000,000 tons, and your midsummer campaign of starvation and slander against your men will give you a saving of $20,000,000 in the cost of mining it.

The paid-up capital of the coal company is $2,500,000. At that figure, as the annual capacity is 1,000,000 to 1,500,000 tons, the saving of ten cents a ton will of itself pay a yearly dividend of 4@6 per cent. on the whole of it. No wonder that your bashaw confidently announced that he would keep the mines closed a year, two years, as many years as needed, and that, if needed, he would make the grass grow in the streets.

You who own the coal company could afford even a longer idleness. Time cannot take away your coal, nor your lots, nor the railroad; but it began, the day after the lock-out, to eat away the hearts and homes, souls and bodies, loves and lives of the poor ones from whom you had determined to steal the $20,000,000 by the brute force of your millions and monopolies.

Mankind shuddered when Louis XIV. gave the order that the Palatinate, alien to him in race and religion, be ravaged. What will the public, to which you appeal, say of you when they comprehend the true nature of the ruin you have visited for your " profit " on men, women, and children of your own country, fellow-citizens, and your " partners " ?

What has been done at Spring Valley is not an extreme case; it has simply been given extra publicity. It is a perfect illustration of our monopolistic morals. You owners of Spring Valley have simply pushed a little farther than poorer men would have dared to do, the principles of buying cheap and selling dear, and the manipulation of the " Eternal law " of supply and demand. The Spring Valley case is only a well-illustrated instance, which shows how rapidly the industry of this country is passing out of the control of business men into that of business animals, whose prototypes must be sought among the carnivora that go on all fours, and who need, as Emerson said of similar men of his time, to be educated out of the quadruped state. The majority of our business men are being consumed, as well as the workingmen, by such monsters. The workingmen feel the devouring tooth of " monopoly " more keenly and more promptly than business men, simply because they are weaker, and have a narrower margin between themselves and death. Prescience should arouse among business men an even sharper ferment of reform than distress has created among the workingmen. Busi-

ness men should make common cause with the
workingmen.   Only by such a coöperation
can the country be saved from the catastrophe
toward which its rights, prosperity, and liberties are being hurried by the greed and lust
of a small body of the richest and most danger-
ously disloyal men popular government has
ever been threatened by

CHAPTER XIII.

THE trouble between you and your men at Spring Valley is one of the incidents of a social war which is raging in the soft coal regions. In this civil strife the mine-owners and railroads of Pennsylvania, Ohio, Indiana and Illinois are fighting with each other, and with the workingmen. It is part of the history of this calamitou struggle that the workingmen have opposed it, and have advocated an enlightened policy of coöperation, which, if the capitalist and corporations had been as civilized, would have put an end to the industrial war with its incalculable losses — losses in life, as well as in property. It is a significant fact that it was at the suggestion of the workingmen that a joint organization of mine-owners or operators, and miners was formed in 1885, which for three years established peace in this industry. On this subject the following from the report on the coal-miners' strike and lock-out in northern Illinois, by J. M. Gould and Fred. H. Wines, special commissioners appointed by the governor, August, 1889 (page 10), is of interest:

"The executive board of the ' National Federation of Miners and Mine-Laborers,' in session at Indianapolis, September 12, 1885, issued an address requesting the mine operators of the United States to meet with said board, ' for the purpose of adjusting the market and mining prices in such a way as to avoid strikes and lock-outs, and give to each party an increased profit from the sale of coal.'

"At a convention held in Chicago, October 15, 1885, at which both operators and miners were present, this call by the miners alone was indorsed, and a joint committee of three operators and three miners was appointed to invite the coöperation of all engaged in coal-mining in America, and to call a meeting of operators and miners in joint convention at Pittsburgh, on the 15th of December, 1885.

"At the Pittsburgh convention a scale of prices for Pennsylvania, Ohio, Indiana, and Illinois was drafted, which was afterward approved by the ' First Annual Joint Conference of Miners and Operators ' at Columbus, Ohio, in February, 1886. This scale was known as the Pittsburgh scale.

"The scale was revised at the second annual conference, also at Columbus, in February, 1887.

"It was again revised at the third annual conference at Pittsburgh, in February, 1888."

This movement to substitute the methods of reason for those of force became abortive through the failure of the operators — employers — to sustain it.   The mine-owners of southern Illinois refused to enter the organization. Those of northern Illinois consequently withdrew in 1888, and the final disruption was brought about in 1889, by the withdrawal of the Indiana operators. The movement was started by the workingmen and loyally supported by them, but killed by the business and railroad men.   In southern Illinois, the miners, despite the hostility of the operators, did their best to establish the system, and through their union succeeded in advancing wages to the figure set for their district by the joint convention.   The workingmen were faithful in all instances.   But the Grape Creek Coal Company of Illinois, although one of the parties to the scale, after agreeing to it, refused to accept it, and kept their men out of work for two years, until at the end of one of the most righteous and obstinate labor strikes on record the men were compelled to give in.   Such

action as this, and the failure of the mine-
owners of southern Illinois to join the movement, and the withdrawal of the northern
Illinois and Indiana operators brought this
most hopeful effort for industrial peace to a
close. The differing attitudes of the workingmen and the employers show the difference in
their philosophy produced by the difference in
their circumstances. The workingman represents the multitude — the people. He knows
by a sure instinct that war is fatal to his welfare. The business man represents the few
who aspire to supremacy over the many by
war. He welcomes the struggle, with all its
chances, for one of these chances is that he
may win great wealth, and be elevated above
all his associates. The workingman stands
for the democratic principle in business ; the
capitalist for the aristocratic.

Behind the failures of the peace movement
in the coal industry, may be easily seen the
malign influence of the railroads. Space for-
bids to give the details here, but broadly, the
refusal of the southern Illinois mines to enter
was because by doing so they and the railroads
with which they are interlinked would have lost
the advantage of making secret and unfair freight
rates. The withdrawal of the northern Illinois

mines had a similar element in it. At the opening of the Pittsburgh conference of 1888, a
leading operator boldly charged that there had
been a " conspiracy between the railway officials
of the Northwestern railroads and the operators of the Northwestern mines of Illinois to
shut out of the great markets of the Northwest, as far as they were able, the coal mined
in Pennsylvania and in Ohio."

The principal owners of the important coal
mines are often owners and officials of the allied
railroads, and they believed they could do
better in a demoralized market, with the help
of " rebates," than they could by assenting to
any open and harmonious arrangement to
settle prices and wages. They might be the
" fittest " who would survive the general ruin.
The baleful disorganizing " rebate " appears
again in the closing scene, when at the last
joint convention, that at Columbus, March 12,
1889, the Indiana operators withdrew. From
the debates in the last joint convention, it is
apparent that the mine-owners of Indiana
calculated that they could make more money
by breaking up this arrangement than by
perpetuating it. If they withdrew from the
mutual obligations it imposed on them with
respect to their competitors of Ohio and

Pennsylvania, who still remained, and their employés, they could have recourse to two sources of profit.   First, they could obtain from the railroads that connected them with Chicago such discriminating freight rates as to give them an insuperable advantage in the market; second, they could whipsaw down the wages of their miners to almost any point by the use of the unemployed labor, so plentiful on all hands.   They withdrew, and the joint convention, after four years' existence, adjourned *sine die*.   In an eloquent speech,* begging the operators and miners not to separate, Col. W. P. Rend said:

It is not for the interest alone of the miners that a settlement should be reached.   It is not for the interests of the operator alone that a settlement should be reached.   It is for the interest of both. It is for the interest of the great principle of conciliation that, for the first time, I believe, in the industrial history of the country, has been given effect to by the miners and operators. * * * It is apparent that this question has got to be settled by one of two methods.   We have got to employ one of two agencies : the agency of force or reason.   Gentlemen, which shall we employ?   Shall we resort to brutal strikes and lock-outs again?   Is that your wish?   Is it the wish of any operator here to go back to the old system; to the old plan of fighting the miners, the plan that entails loss of capital, the plan which brings with it oftentimes scenes of bloodshed and disorder to the State, and which engenders feelings of enmity and hatred

---

* From the official verbatim report of the Fourth Annual Joint Conference of Miners and Operators held at Indianapolis, February 5-7, and Columbus, March 12-14, 1889.   (Pages 112, 113, 114, 115.)

between capital and labor? I do not believe that you want to go back to that old system. The other system is that of reason and intelligence, of using the highest power and the highest faculty that God Almighty has given us. Three or four years ago we decided that the agency of reason was the proper one for us to employ. We met together; operators and miners both raised their voice in condemnation of the system of strikes that had characterized, and I might say brutalized, the industry before. After a great deal of discussion and several conferences, we found a common standing ground. We formulated scales. We established peace, we established concord, we established good-will, where before there had been either open warfare or an unfriendly peace, and where before there had been discord, enmity and hatred. We have accomplished marvelous results, gentlemen, during the last three years. I do not think that the most sanguine of the originators of this plan had believed that such grand results could be accomplished in such a short time. Now, gentlemen, it is not necessary for me to delay you in going over the history of our dealings during the past three years. Suffice it to say that we are convinced of the wisdom and justice of the principles of arbitration.

     *   *   *   When this movement was first organized it was treated with ridicule. It had no friends. Many of the operators of the United States looked upon it as averse to their interests. They said: "Gentlemen, you will build up a gigantic Miners' Union, that will use its strength to make war upon us." "You are giving strength to the enemy," they said. I did not believe it. A great many of them called it a delusion. They said: "It is an impossibility for so many interests to agree where there is such a conflict and such a complication of interests. It is impossible to adopt any scale or any general arrangement between operators and miners." Where it was not looked upon as folly, it was regarded by many operators as a vague chimera. We have demonstrated by three years' trial and experience that it has been a strength to the cause of capital; it has helped capital. (Applause.) Gentlemen, no

man here in this room, I believe, representing the operators, will deny the fact that the last three years have been the best period that we have experienced in the entire history of the coal trade. You have derived a benefit from it. I have been benefited by it, and it is useless, it is false, for any man to get up and say that this movement has been injurious to the interests of capital. It has been a benefit to the interests of capital and labor, and you have both been benefited by this peaceful mode of settlement. Before this, as I said before, there was a general feeling of hostility. We looked upon one another as enemies. We did not understand one another, gentlemen. We did not understand each other's position. The miner felt that he was a victim of wrong, of grave oppression. He felt that capital was a hard taskmaster, that ground him down. He felt justified, whenever an opportunity presented itself where he could take advantage of his employer, in taking that advantage. The pain of his suffering became more intense, from the belief that his employer was the cause of his privation and misery. On the other hand, the operator looked upon the miner as unreasoning, and as turbulent. He felt that no matter what concessions he made, no matter what he did, no matter what act of kindness he would extend, he would be rewarded with ingratitude. These opinions were largely false, and due to misconceptions. Their falsity has become apparent from the happy experience of the past three years. We have now become acquainted, and mutually understand each others' purposes and sentiments. The men we have met here — I say it with no idea of flattery, no idea of currying any favors; I ask no favors of any man (Applause)— but I say that the men we have come here to meet, we feel it an honor to meet. They are men of intelligence; they are thoughtful men, and they mean to act fairly and justly. They state their case fairly, and they argue it well. We find they are better equipped and better prepared with arguments than we are. We find able men here representing the miners. We are proud to meet men of this kind. Now we are dealing with intelligence, where oftentimes before we had to deal with ignorance. Sound sense, good judgment and a spirit of fairness characterize the demands and claims here presented by the miners' delegates."

The break-down of the joint organization of miners and operators was followed by a season of strikes and lock-outs, ending in great losses to all, and in reductions of wages to the miners; but the problem of organizing for the common good, thus selfishly abandoned by the capitalists, has been taken up again by the workingmen. After the lock-out and strikes of the soft-coal region were over, President John McBride, of the Miners' Progressive Union, issued the following call for a convention of five States:

NATIONAL PROGRESSIVE UNION MINERS
AND MINE LABORERS,
GEN. OFFICE, COLUMBUS, Nov 18, 1889.

The miners of northern Illinois, Indiana, Ohio, western Illinois, western Pennsylvania and West Virginia, whose coal goes into Western and Northwestern markets, are hereby notified that a convention of this competitive district will be held in Indianapolis, Ind., at 10 A. M., on Wednesday, December 18, 1889.

All miners not organized are requested to meet at their respective mines to select and send delegates to this convention.

The objects of this convention will be to consider and determine upon a policy by and through which the interests of the miners and mine laborers may be better protected and their wages advanced during the coming year.

The joint movement of operators and miners for the adjustment of mining rates in this district gave good results to both

14

parties while it lasted, but the withdrawal of Illinois and Indiana operators from the movement and the bitter warfare waged by them since May last against their employés makes it practically impossible for us to meet them in convention next spring.

The experience of the last six months proves to us that miners in no one or two States in this district should again enter into an agreement with their employers and allow miners in other sections of the district to do all the striking. We must stand or fall together as a district.

We prefer peace rather than contention with the operators, but the good of our craftsmen in this field now depends that we either secure a general agreement or depend upon our own efforts to win just and equitable rates and conditions. The latter, judging from present surroundings, seems inevitable during the coming year, hence we advise the consideration of a policy that will include, among other things :

1. Restriction either in hours, tonnage or by a series of suspensions at stated intervals throughout the entire competitive district.

2. The creation of a large defense fund between this and May 1, 1890, to be used for the carrying out of the policy agreed upon by the convention.

The conditions of the coal market now warrant better prices than are being paid for mining, and, if our judgment is not seriously at fault, next year will increase the prosperity of the coal mining industry. It will be our own fault if we do not receive better returns for labor performed next year.

We now ask that each miner do his duty, and urge immediate election of delegates. Fraternally yours,

JOHN McBRIDE, Prest.

In opening the convention, called as above, President McBride said, among other things :

The history of the "joint movement" in this competitive district during the past four years has clearly demonstrated that in an intellectual contest we have been able to hold our own with the owners and operators of mines, and I do not hesitate in saying that, were disputes between mine employers and employés to be adjusted by arbitration, instead of by a resort to strikes, the ability of your representatives, aided by facts and the logic of the situation, would have retained prices and bettered mining conditions throughout the competitive district; but the discordant and demoralized state our forces were in, together with their weakness financially, seemed to court the destruction of conciliatory methods, and invite a conflict with operators which could not but end in loss and disaster to us.

To relieve the distress of those on strike and to reduce their wants to a minimum, is a duty devolving upon our craftsmen who continue at work, but to our shame it must be said that this duty has been but indifferently discharged in the past by the great majority of those who had work to do, and as a result their fellow-miners who were striking and suffering were compelled to accept defeat, starve or appeal for aid to a sympathetic and charitable public.

If miners and mine laborers would but do their duty toward each other this need not occur ; and I am sick and tired of being humiliated year in and year out by having to publish to the world that my craftsmen are so lacking in energy and enterprise that, rather than make proper financial provisions in time of peace to protect their interests during periodical and apparently inevitable wage contests, they prefer to be classed as paupers and mendicants. This language may sound severe and harsh to you — it certainly is not pleasant to me — but it is true, and we are forcibly reminded of its truth by the fact that during the several months' strike of the nine thousand miners and mine laborers in Indiana and Illinois only about forty thousand dollars in money and goods was contributed to aid them. This would be but a small amount for the more than sixty thousand mine workers of this competitive district to pay, but the records show that fully one-half of this sum was contributed by others than mine workers, and this showing is not creditable to us.

No wonder that operators so loudly boasted of their ability to starve their miners into submission.

The convention adopted the following resolutions:

WHEREAS, The almost total defeat of the miners of Northern Illinois and in the block coal fields of Indiana has caused them to lose by cessation of work for six months, and by reduced wages for the next six months, at least half a million dollars, and to this may be added the amount of money contributed by those not engaged in the strike; and,

WHEREAS, The miners in other parts of the competitive field are now in danger of having prices and conditions similar to Indiana and Illinois forced upon them; to prevent such a calamity, mine workers of the entire district must decide, and decide quickly, to cease complaining about their inability to live upon their meager earnings, and purpose to make a mutual and determined fight along the line by contributions of a few dollars each to a fund that will be large enough to guarantee the success of a strike inaugurated to restore, not alone the old rates in Illinois and Indiana, but an increased price throughout the entire field. This must be done, or all go down to a lower level. Therefore, be it

Resolved, That we favor the creation of a fund large enough for both offensive and defensive purposes, and with this end in view we recommend that mine workers throughout the entire competitive district be assessed $1 per month for the months of February, March and April, the sum to be paid into the general treasury; and

Resolved, That we advise our mine workers of this district to consider, that, if an amount equal to one-half the money lost through the failure of the late strikes was centered in a general fund, it would prevent defeat in future contests for wage adjustment. Be it further

Resolved, That the mine workers of this district instruct their delegates to the national convention, to be held in Colum-

bes, Ohio, at an early date, to vote for or against the creation
of such a general fund by the methods herein advised, and to
also provide for the election of a board of trustees and proper
safeguards to prevent the misuse of any part of the funds for
purposes other than those for which it is asked to be created.

WHEREAS, The reports of the delegates show that the
miners represented are almost unanimous in their desire to have
the eight-hour day imposed in the competitive district, either on
May 1, 1890, or as soon thereafter as practicable, therefore,
be it

Resolved, That we ask the miners and mine workers in this
competitive field to prepare to put the eight-hour day in force
on May 1, 1890, and that our delegates to the Columbus convention urge the co-operation of miners.

Resolved, That we are in favor of a restriction in the output
of coal in this competitive field and leave to the Columbus Convention to determine the best method of restriction and the
time it shall take effect.

Resolved, That this convention urge the miners of Illinois to
use every available means to establish a shorter interval between
pay days.

If there has been any movement among the
operators toward organization, it has not been
public, like all the proceedings of the miners.
But it is not likely any such movement has
been attempted. The forces at work among
the capitalists, are forces of selfishness and
disintegration, not of union for mutual benefit.
A desperate struggle is on for the partition of
the soft coal business of the country among the
leading railroads and their business favorites.
The interests of the miners, of the operators,
and of the public, must all stand in abeyance

until this process of coal monopolization is settled. If it is settled by the survival of the "fittest" of these anarchical contestants, it will be found too late that another American industry has passed under the absolute control of a few men. These men will be able to fix by the tariffs of a few railroad managers, and by the votes of a half-dozen trustees, what men shall be permitted to own and operate coal mines, how much coal shall be mined each year, what mines shall be operated, which closed, what price the public shall pay, what wages the miners shall receive, and at what points the industry of America dependent on fuel shall or shall not be permitted to expand. The men who have this power in the coal market will have much to say, also, along with similar lords of industry in other markets, about who shall be senator, president, judge, what laws shall be enacted, and how taxes shall be apportioned among the people. Only a fool can suppose that the republic of the United States of America will survive the continuance of such a system as this, which before our eyes is being set up in the most important departments of the life of the American people.

CHAPTER XIV.

FIRST FRUITS — WHAT WILL THE LAST BE?

BONAMY PRICE, then Professor of Political Economy at Oxford, visiting Chicago, called about himself a parlorful of people, and asked this question: " What is it specially distinguishes man from the brute? " There were many answers, but his own was the only one he liked: " Progressive desire. Like Oliver Twist, man is always crying for more." By virtue of this law, man, when associated as a railroad, continually reaches out for more, more railroad, more power. The locomotive is the representative of our age. Concentrated in it are all the tendencies of our civilization in their intensest culmination. It stands for the millionaire and the tramp, the overworked " hand," and the laborer displaced by machinery, the corporation dominating the state, the idolatry of the god of our day — the bargain. Steam and machinery reach their climax in the locomotive. The commercial fanaticism of the right to do what one wills with his own, and

to buy and sell anything, has found in the locomotive the potent instrument which rides
over all the rights of the people in highways,
businesses, courts and government, and drowns
all protest with its screaming doctrine, that
public roads are private property, and that
private property is the government of the
many by the few, " of divine right," and not
to be questioned. This control of the highways tends to become the control of the country dependent on the highway, and of all the
men and things therein. The framers of the
last constitution of Pennsylvania, knowing this,
sought to counteract this dangerous tendency
in the field where it was foreseen it might produce its most calamitous effects, by forbidding
any railroad to own or operate coal mines.
But, as they at the same time neglected to
make it impossible for the railroads to become
the owners of the courts and legislatures,
through which this prohibition was to be enforced, the wise foresight was of no avail. The
sole effect of this provision of the constitution
has been that the railroads became the owners
in fee simple (very simple) of the government
of the state, as well as of the forbidden coal
fields. To-day a few law-breaking, anarchy-
practicing railroad giants, with a few enor-

mously wealthy individuals bound to them
by invisible but unbreakable money-belts,
own all the hard coal fields of the great State
of Pennsylvania. In the language of the congressional report on the labor troubles in
Pennsylvania, in 1888, " seven coal-carrying
railroads, which are at the same time coal
miners, may be said to own or control all the
anthracite of the United States."

The report further says : " During the first
forty years the mines were worked by individuals, just as are farms. The hundreds of employers were in active competition with each
other for labor. The fundamental law of supply and demand alike governed all parties.
As to engagement, employer and employé
stood upon a common level of equality and
manhood. Skill and industry upon the part
of the miner assured to him steady work, fair
wages, honest measurement, and humane
treatment. Should these be denied by one
employer, many other employers were ready to
give them. The miner had the same freedom
as to engagement, the same reward for faithful
service and protection against injustice, that
the farm hand possesses because of the competition between farmers employing hands.
With the development of the railroad system

and its peculiar methods, the law of competition was steadily restrained, and finally suspended. To-day seven great carrying companies are the real operators in the whole region, and have either driven out the many individual operators or else absolutely control the few that remain. This virtual combination of all employers into one syndicate has practically abolished competition between them as to wages, and gradually but inexorably the workmen have found themselves encoiled as by an anaconda, until now they are powerless."

The law of " progressive desire," which drives the railroads to become the owners of tonnage as well as the movers of it, has been stronger than the law of the land. This law, that the ownership of the highways grows steadily into the ownership of the country dependent on the highways, is to-day to be seen in as active operation in the West as in the East. Nothing produces so much freight to the acre as a good coal mine; no other source of freight is so concentrated, and so easy to control as coal land. No single item of expense in railroading is greater than the supply of coal. No other kind of commodity is so certain always to demand distribution by

the railroads as coal. It is possible to conceive
of each locality in the West turning in upon
itself for the supply of its food; but coal is
found only in spots, and the business of distributing it is one railroad men know the world
will not outgrow. Hence the leading railroads
in the West some years ago began to imitate
the policy so successful in Pennsylvania, despite
the law — the policy of becoming the owners
of their own coal mines. In this way they get
at cost the enormous amounts of coal they use
themselves, and secure on most, if not all, the
coal used by their " provinces," the several
profits of mining, carrying and selling. The
Northern Pacific owns coal mines on the
Pacific coast; the Union Pacific, those at Rock
Spring, Wyoming; the Central Pacific and
Southern Pacific are supplied by their mines.
The Atchison, Topeka & Santa Fé gets coal
for itself and its provinces from its own mines
at Trinidad, Colo.; Pittsburg, Kan., and
other points. The Braceville, Ill., coal
mines are the adjunct of the Chicago, Milwaukee & St. Paul. If the Chicago, Burlington & Quincy did not own its own coal mines,
it bought some of its supplies from mines owned
by leading stockholders. Similar arrangements have been made by the Illinois Central,

the Chicago & Alton, the Chicago & Rock Island, the Wabash; by the Chicago & North-Western at other points — as in Iowa — than at Spring Valley, and by other railroads.

It would require a more intimate acquaintance with the inner mysteries of the great railroads than outsiders usually have, to be able to say with certainty in what cases coal mines are really owned by the corporations in connection with which they are operated. Sometimes they are owned by " rings " of the managers, who thereby acquire the pleasing and profitable power — nothing could ever give them the right — of buying as officials of the railroad, from themselves as individuals. This works to the great advantage of the individual, who has great luck in getting good bargains out of the official. We see here, no doubt, one of the reasons why all our great business geniuses make such point of the sacredness of " individual enterprise." The mines from which the Missouri Pacific and its allied roads draw their fuel and coal freight are understood to be largely the property of the distinguished professor of the science of " individual enterprise," who has been in control for many years of that main highway of the Southwest. The "evolution " — to give a respectable name to the proceedings of so highly respectable men — which has made the property of the many the property of the few, and has converted yeomen into miners, and miners into slaves in the hard-coal fields, is already well under way in the soft-coal districts. Good society meets the poor reformer with the angry charge that he means to divide up property, but it winks complacently upon the commercial monsters who are visibly dividing the property of their neighbors and competitors among themselves. All the evil features of the destruction of private property and personal liberty in Pennsylvania are being repeated in the coal regions of the West, as illustrated in the rapid monopolization of the vast coal deposits by comparatively a few men controlling rates of transportation, and by the misery and degradation forced upon whole communities like yours of Spring Valley, and like Brazil, Braidwood, the Hocking Valley, and other places.

In this first short half-century the enthusiasts for improved transportation who so humbly begged the State for charters to permit them to take away other men's land without their consent, for little experimental railroads, and who so thankfully solicited and re-

ceived every gift of bonds, lands, money or
" county aid," have grown to be these giants,
getting from the strong meat of highway
monopoly the strength to reach out for land
monopoly and market monopoly. If these are
the fruits of the first fifty years, what will be
those of the next fifty years? If these are the
winnings of the inaugural era which has seen
only the consolidations of local lines into trunk
lines, what will be the winnings of the period
already begun, which will be signalized by the
union of the trunk lines into one or two great
railway trusts, operated by private citizens for
private profit, claiming the highways of the
nation as private property, and using this private property as the jimmy with which to get
possession of all other property?

If the fuel famines of Kansas and Dakota, if
the extortions of the coal rings and trusts of
Chicago and Pennsylvania, if the ruin of Spring
Valley, if the pitiable poverty of the miners of
Pennsylvania, if the extermination of the individual coal-mine owners of Pennsylvania and
Illinois, and the " division of property" taken
from them, among their powerful destroyers,
if these denials of the " sacred right to work "
and of " private property" are the fruits of
these first years, when these properties and

privileges are still managed by men who have
sprung from the people, what will the fruits be
in the second and third generations, when all
this power has passed into the hands of those
who, by experience, education and habits of
life belong to another world than the com-
monalty, and who have acquired a taste for
powers and luxury that must be satisfied by
greater and greater levies on the people? If
these are the fruits of the grasping of coal
mines by the owners of the highways, and the
Napoleons of commercial conquest, what will
be the fruits of their ownership of the other
mines, the forests, and the factories, and farms,
all of which must in time be surrendered to
the " progressive desire " of the lords of industry?

CHAPTER XV.

PART OF THE MORAL.

MEN do not lose nor lessen their personal responsibility by acting through a corporation, or an agent, or by any other indirection. The growing shrewdness of the public will only lay a surer and heavier hand on those who smite their brothers from behind that ancient and uncanny creature — the corporate person — and then claim immunity for their souls and bodies, because their dummy has no body to be kicked, and no soul to be damned. Of the two leading authorities on the law of American corporations, Taylor says:*

" It is the opinion of the writer that the fiction of the ' legal person ' has outlived its usefulness, and is no longer adequate for the purposes of an accurate treatment of the legal relations† arising through the prosecution of a corporate enterprise. By dismissing this fic-

---

* Preface to " Law of Private Corporations," by H. O. Taylor. Philadelphia: Kay & Bros., 1884.
† Or moral or economic.

tion a clearer view may be had of the actual human beings interested, whose rights may then be determined without unnecessary mystification;" and Morawetz says:*

"The existence of a corporation as an entity independently of its members is a fiction; * * * while the fiction of a corporate entity has important uses and cannot be dispensed with, it is nevertheless essential to bear in mind distinctly that the rights and duties of an incorporated association are in reality the rights and duties of the persons who compose it, and not of an imaginary being."

What men do in managing enterprises chartered by the public is not "their private business." In such affairs they are public functionaries doing the business of the public.

Such men as public functionaries are as lawfully and inevitably to be called before the people by name for the public discussion and criticism of their acts as any other public servants. "For, although," says Ruskin, "many of my discreet friends cry out upon me for allowing 'personalities,' it is my firm conviction that only by justly personal direction of

---

* "Law of Private Corporations," by Victor Morawetz. Boston: Little, Brown & Co., 1886.

15

blame can any abuse be vigorously dealt with."

He who acquires profits or property is responsible for all the means that produced them. Ignorance of this law excuses no man.

Step by step the " Model Merchant" has pushed his right to buy cheap and sell dear far beyond the necessary limitations of law, economy, morals and humanity.

Modern business under the leadership of the Captains of Industry has developed into an unnatural fanaticism of greed, producing a seditious wealth and a morbid poverty.

Under the inspiration of this fanaticism, men irreproachable in other relations of life proclaim and practice their right to consume the livelihood, the liberties and even the lives of their fellow-citizens in order to multiply superfluities of power and luxury for themselves.

These fanatics of business — few but supreme — set a pace which is leading our business civilization to destruction.

That the·sort of thing you have done at Spring Valley, and others like you have done in the valleys of Pennsylvania, Ohio, Indiana, and elsewhere, will be made conspiracy by law if necessary, is certain as soon as the public get to grasp the motive and the result of such concerted attacks upon the lives and liberties of the people. It will be in vain that you who own and manage the North-Western Railroad will repel with indignation and amazement the charge that you are in any way responsible. You did not know what was being done? You have accepted and continue ready to accept its result. You only built a railroad to a coal field, as any one might do, and are not responsible for any wrong committed in the production of the coal of which you were only the carrier? Your position is infinitely worse than that. Owners and managers with you in the railroad were owners and managers of the coal company and land company, and your acts disclose a concert of action with a common purpose in the co-opperated management of those properties. The question of conspiracy is a question of circumstantial evidence, and of the public judgment of the evidence to be expressed, it is to be hoped, some day by a jury, in the " good old times " that are coming, when the public wits will have developed to the point of taking away from the poor and lowly their present monopoly of conspiracy. The building of the road and the booming of the town went on together under the direction of a mutual ele-

ment in both companies.   When the dooming
of the town began, you of the railroad submitted to it and to the loss of heavy traffic
receipts, when by a word you could have compelled your other selves of the coal company
to have continued the mining and supply of
coal.   Now that the people have been starved
into surrender, you have put on your trains
again and use the coal again.   You will boast
again in your annual report, as you have done,
of the progressive cheapness per ton of your
coal—$2.28 a ton in 1885, $1.96 in 1886,
$1.75 in 1887, and perhaps $1.50 this year—
a progressive cheapness every downward cent
in which represents scores of broken lives.
The railroad has made prices on Spring Valley
coal at competitive points which indicate rebates on its transportation.   High officials of
the freight department of the road have
appeared in person at the public tender of
bids for the supply of Spring Valley coal to
public institutions in competition with other
coals.   This cumulation of evidence tells its
own story.   Nor can you of the coal company
protect yourselves by the plea that competition forced you to do what you did.   The
facts given above about the wages paid by
your competitors, and your own latest offers,

take that ground from under you. But waiving all that, you have no right to create such competition, and then plead it as an excuse for other wrongs.

If you continue your war on the miners, if you pocket the profits that success will bring you, the public will sooner or later declare to all of you that you have vitiated your title to your rights and properties at their very roots. Political economy gives you private property only that the interest of all may be served by your self-interest; the law gives you your franchises and estates only for the general welfare and the public safety; religion holds you to be only stewards of your riches. If you usurp for your private profit all these trusts and grants, if you withdraw yourself from serving and protecting the public and take to oppressing and plundering them from your points of advantage, you will but repeat the folly of your mediæval exemplars whose castles now decorate a better civilization with their prophetic ruins.

APPENDIX.

THE first and last statement to the public by the Spring Valley Coal Company after the lock-out of December and May, was in the following letter to Governor Fifer. It was made to justify the offer of August 23d of ostensibly 75, really 35 cents a ton.

Hon. Joseph W. Fifer, Governor of the State of Illinois.

SIR—The undersigned, in behalf of himself and those connected with him in the ownership and control of the Spring Valley Coal Company, respectfully submits to you, and through you to the public, the following statement of facts, which can be verified and confirmed by evidence and figures which we ask you and the public to impartially consider in refutation of the uncalled-for and unjust abuse which the managers of the company's property have been subjected to.

The Spring Valley Coal Company was organized under the laws of the State of Illinois in the year 1884 to develop a coal territory north of the Illinois River, about 100 miles southwest of Chicago, which field embraces about 40,000 acres. Within this territory, in 1884, there were two small mines in operation, supplying the local demands of the neighborhood, the total output of these mines not then exceeding 500 tons per day. As to

(230)

the value of this coal field I can submit no better evidence than the fact that no coal operator in your State was willing to risk his money in its development and improvement, or considered it of sufficient value to invest one dollar in it. Neither myself nor my associates supposed, when we concluded to try and utilize this coal property and develop it, that we were committing any crime. We supposed, that, so long as we conformed to the laws of the State of Illinois and obeyed them, we would be protected in our lawful rights, including the right of controlling our property to the extent that other corporations and citizens of your State enjoy. We asked for nothing more; we are entitled to nothing less. In this supposition we have found ourselves sadly mistaken. Venal and partisan newspapers, as well as politicians, desiring to serve political ends, together with a few honest and charitable citizens and misguided clergymen, have, without the necessary facts or knowledge to enable them to form a correct opinion, heaped upon this company and its officers, through the press, an amount of falsehood and slander that is perhaps without parallel in the industrial history of this country.

The development of the Spring Valley coal field was not engaged in for speculative purposes. All we could hope for was a very moderate return on the capital invested. The Spring Valley Coal Company purchased the coal rights and lands in fee now owned by it located in the counties of Bureau, La Salle, and Putnam, paying to the farmers of those counties something over $650,000 for the same, and of this sum $350,000 to $400,-000 was utilized by them in removing mortgages from the land, the surface of which they retained. The company up to date has further expended a large amount of money in improving and developing the property, and to-day our mines have the capacity to produce over 4,000 tons of coal per day, when in operation — a capacity exceeding that of any other mines in the world worked under the long-wall system. You can readily understand, sir, that a property capable of producing from 1,000,000 to 1,500,-000 tons of coal per annum could not expect to find a market for its coal locally, situated as the Spring Valley Coal Company

is, but from necessity would have to look to the States and Territories of the North and Northwest to market its product. The
ability of the company to operate its mines, to give steady employment to its men, and to sell its coal, is contingent upon two
factors — first, the cost of mining at Spring Valley, as compared
with the cost at the mines in the other Illinois coal fields with
which we come in competition; second, the cost of railroad
transportation from Spring Valley to competitive markets as
compared with the cost of transportation from mines in the
other fields to the same markets. The coal fields with which
the Spring Valley Company has to compete virtually embrace
the entire coal area of the State of Illinois south of the Illinois
River at Spring Valley, and extending to within forty-five miles
of St. Louis. Within this field are located what are known as
the Streator, Braidwood, and Wilmington districts, constituting
a part of what are known as the northern Illinois coal field.
Taking Streator as the center of this group of mines in the
northern field, and St. Paul, Minn., as a market for Illinois
coal, the relative distance from Spring Valley to St. Paul is
twenty miles less than from Streator. As you go south and
southwest on the lines of the railroads from Chicago, extending
into what are known as the central and southern coal fields of
Illinois, there are numerous mines producing and shipping coal
into the Chicago market and the markets of the Northwest; and,
if we take Essex, on the line of the Wabash road, which is the
transfer point of coal from these central and southern fields, and
Chicago and St. Paul as competitive markets, we find the distance from Spring Valley to Chicago is 101 miles, and to St.
Paul, by the shortest route, 420 miles, as against 60 miles from
Essex to Chicago and 470 miles from Essex to St. Paul.

Under an arrangement between the railroads of your State,
centering in Chicago and extending into the North and Northwest, within which territory the northern Illinois coal mines
are solely dependent for a market for their product, the following system and rates of transportation have been adopted and
are to-day in force: A zone or territory embracing certain coal
fields in northern, central, and southern Illinois has been estab-

lished, and the rates of railroad transportation upon coal from all mines within this zone, passing through and going beyond Chicago by rail lines from Chicago, are uniform, irrespective of the distance the coal is transported from points within this zone to Chicago. The limits of this zone are as follows: Starting from the city of Chicago due west to Clinton, Iowa, thence following the Mississippi River as far south as Burlington; thence in a southeasterly direction, passing through Bushnell and Vermont; thence in a northeasterly direction through Peoria, Lacon, Minonk, and Essex to Chicago; embracing all the mines and coal deposits within the territory described. The southern limit of this zone or belt is Vermont, distant from Chicago 211 miles, and from St. Paul, via Chicago, 621 miles by the shortest rail route; as compared from Spring Valley to Chicago, 101 miles, and St. Paul 420 miles. But, perhaps, Peoria is a better illustration, for the reason that larger shipments of competitive coal are sold in the Chicago market and markets of the Northwest from the mines in that vicinity. The price of mining in the Peoria mines last year was sixty cents a ton, as against ninety cents paid at Spring Valley. The distance from Peoria to Chicago is 161 miles, and from Peoria to St. Paul, via Chicago, 571 miles. Now, a ton of coal shipped from Peoria to St. Paul, via Chicago, a distance of 571 miles, pays only the same rate per ton for transportation that a ton of Spring Valley coal pays for 420 miles, with a difference of over thirty-five cents per ton in cost of mining in favor of Peoria.

To further illustrate the inequalities of railroad transportation affecting the operation of the fields of northern Illinois, we would refer to the Consolidated Coal Company's mines, operated within fifty-four miles of St. Louis, with a claimed production of 10,000 tons per day. The actual amount paid for the transportation of a ton of coal by the Consolidated Coal Company from their mines to St. Paul is $2.40, as against $2 from Spring Valley to St. Paul; but the distance from the Consolidated mines to St. Paul is 636 miles, while from Spring Valley to St. Paul it is 420 miles, and an equivalent rate for a ton of coal from Spring Valley to St. Paul would be $1.58 per ton, as against the $2.40 paid on a ton of coal from the Consolidated mines, or a discrimination against Spring Valley, on the distance relatively transported, of forty-two cents per ton; and the price paid for mining a ton of coal at the Consolidated mines is forty-five cents, as against ninety cents a ton paid at Spring Valley.   This coal to-day is sold in the city of Chicago for $1.65 per ton, and is sold at Essex for $1.25 per ton.

Now as to the relative cost of mining a ton of coal at Spring Valley as compared with the cost of mining at other mines in the northern field, and with the fields of central and southern Illinois: Since the Spring Valley Coal Company has been in operation the price paid the miners for mining a ton of coal has been uniformly 90 cents per ton, with sixteen inches of brushing, as against an average price of 80 cents a ton paid for mining a ton of coal in the other mines of the northern coal field, as against 60 cents and as low as 45 cents a ton paid for mining in the central and southern coal fields.

(As the general public may not understand the meaning of the term "brushing" used in this letter, I would state that it refers to the refuse rock or other material overlying or underlying the vein of coal, and where a vein of coal is not of sufficient thickness, when mined, to leave a perpendicular space high enough to permit a pit car to reach the face of the vein, of sufficient capacity to haul a maximum load of coal to the bottom of the shaft, this material either overlying or underlying the vein of coal has to be removed to secure the necessary height, and this refuse necessary to be removed is what is technically known as "brushing.")

There has been no period during the four years which we have operated the Spring Valley mines that we could not purchase, and, in fact, we have purchased, coal from other mines in the northern field at from 12 cents to $17\frac{1}{2}$ cents per ton less than the actual cost of producing the coal at our own property; and, as the rates of transportation from these fields from Chicago and St. Paul were the same that our company had to pay, I think you will agree with me that we could hardly expect to be able to maintain ourselves in a competitive market.   But we have gone on hoping for a better condition of affairs, when we would be able to keep our works going and our men employed, and we stopped work only when the men declined to meet us to endeavor to agree upon a price to be paid for mining for the present year, and when we found that it was an utter impossibility for us to continue operations without virtually bankrupting our company. The mild winter of 1888–89 so affected the demand for coal that in December we were compelled to shut down two of our mines, as there was no market for the coal ; and for reasons hereafter explained, we were compelled to shut down the remainder of the mines May 1st, following.

About the 1st of April, and prior to deciding to close the mines, I was advised by our superintendent that a committee representing our miners desired to meet me in Chicago and see if some equitable basis of mining could be agreed upon for the then ensuing year. I was then in the city of New York, and went from there to Chicago in compliance with this request, and was there on the day fixed by the committee. I remained in Chicago two days, and during that time a telegraphic notice was received from this committee that they would not come to Chicago. This notice on their part being equivalent to abandoning the idea of having a conference, I returned home and ordered the works closed on the following 1st of May, on which date all the other mines in the northern field ceased to work, demanding a reduction in the price of mining.

We have never asked, expected, or desired a miner working in our mines to mine coal for us at one cent a ton less than a fair relative price as compared with what was paid in other fields in northern Illinois. As every intelligent coal operator and miner knows, in fixing a rate for mining coal there are advantages and disadvantages to be found in the same veins, even in the same field, which must be taken into consideration in arriving at what are fair and practically equal prices to be paid for mining at the different mines in such field. It would be clearly unreasonable to expect, and unjust to ask, miners to mine coal at Spring Valley at the same price paid for mining in the Braidwood field if it can be shown that the disadvantages at Spring Valley are greater than those at Braidwood; and, of course, the foregoing applies equally to Braidwood if the conditions be reversed.

There is not in the State of Illinois, nor in the United States, a coal property where men can work with less discomfort and greater safety to life and limb than they can in the Spring Valley mines. During the four years that the mines have been in operation, not one life has been lost. The mines are practically free from water, which fact inures greatly to the comfort, not only of the miner, but to his ability to mine coal therein.

You are, sir, respectfully asked to compare the price paid for mining at Spring Valley during the last four years with the price paid at Braidwood, at which latter place the highest nominal price per ton was paid during this period for mining coal in the State of Illinois. The basis upon which coal was mined at Braidwood was 80 cents per ton for a vein of coal 2 feet 10 inches thick, and 15 cents per ton additional for a minimum brushing of 3 feet 6 inches and a maximum of 4 feet—the contract between the operators and miners at Braidwood specifying 4 feet. Taking the minimum brushing as the basis, the aggregate price was 95 cents a ton, which covered the cost of mining the coal and brushing of 42 inches. Now, it must be kept in mind in making this comparison that the relative conditions of mining the seams of coal at Braidwood and at Spring Valley are practically the same, except as to the thickness of the veins; and we also claim for Spring Valley certain advantages which do not necessarily come into the actual cost of production, but which are of material advantage to the miner. The percentage of slack and nut coal produced in both veins is the same. The stratum under the veins is the same—namely, fire-clay. Both mines are operated on the long-wall system, consequently the breaking down of the coal in each is the same. The differences which exist in the comparative working of the two veins are, first, the Spring Valley vein is entirely free from water; second, it is practically free from faults; third, the vein lies on a horizontal plane that does not vary from one to three feet in a mile in the level of the coal; fourth, the roof is perfectly dry and of free soapstone rock, 14 feet thick. In the Braidwood district there is a large amount of water, and the dip and rise of the vein in 1,000 yards varies as much as forty feet. The roof at Braidwood is water-soaked, and is much more difficult to maintain, which work has to be done by the men, and is covered in the price paid for mining. In some places the Braidwood vein comes within 25 feet of the surface, while at no point at Spring Valley is the third vein within 450 feet of the surface. These comparative advantages and disadvantages in the working of the two veins, whatever they may be, are largely in favor of the Spring Valley miner. During the last four years we paid our men 90 cents per ton for mining coal, including 16 inches of brushing. We require 30 inches of brushing to enable us to economically mine the coal. Now, it can be readily understood that, if a miner can mine a ton of coal at Braidwood at 80 cents a ton for mining, and 15 cents a ton for 42 inches of brushing — all conditions being equal at both mines, except as to the thickness of the veins — the relative price at Spring Valley for 16 inches of brushing would be 85.71 cents per ton, and in this comparison we do not take into consideration the fact that our vein is 10 inches thicker than the vein at Braidwood.

Now, let the cost of mining at Braidwood be compared with what would be the relative cost of the same work at Spring Valley, and what would be an equivalent price to be paid at Spring Valley as compared with that paid at Braidwood?

An ordinary working place at Braidwood is 42 feet face, 2 feet 10 inches high (of coal), 3 feet deep, with three men working in the face. Now 2 feet 10 inches of coal, 42 feet face, and 3 feet deep, contains 357 cubic feet, and allowing 80 pounds of coal to the cubic foot the space would produce 14 tons and 560 pounds of coal at Braidwood. It must be borne in mind also that the miners claim that it is impracticable for them to work three men in a working place at Spring Valley in a space of 36 feet face; but three men do work in a working place at Braidwood in 2 feet 10 inches of coal, 42 feet face, and there is no objection to it on the part of the men.

It is as feasible and practicable to make the working places at Spring Valley 42 feet (we now work there 36) as it is at Braidwood. If, therefore, the working places should be increased six additional feet, to enable three men to work instead of two, which can be readily done at Spring Valley, a working place at the latter mines with the same working face as at Braidwood — namely, 42 feet face, 3 feet deep, and the thickness of the vein being 3 feet 8 inches — would contain 462 cubic feet, and at 80 pounds of coal per cubic foot would produce 18 tons 960 pounds of coal; or 4 tons and 400 pounds more coal would be produced in the same space at Spring Valley than at Braidwood.

It must be kept in mind, also, that not one additional stroke of a miner's arm is required in connection with the bearing in or breaking down of this 18 tons 960 pounds of coal at Spring Valley over what it requires at Braidwood for 14 tons 560 pounds within the space given.

The foregoing figures show that three men in a working place at Braidwood, working in the space heretofore given, would mine 14 tons 560 pounds of coal, by which, at 95 cents per ton paid at Braidwood, they would earn $13.57, and that for the same work at Spring Valley, in the same space, they would produce 18 tons 960 pounds, which, at 90 cents a ton, the price paid last year, would amount to $16.63, which would be $3.06 more earned by the men at Spring Valley than at Braidwood, which $3.06 would be equivalent to 16.56 cents per ton paid at Spring Valley more than was paid at Braidwood. This excess of earnings by the men at Spring Valley over that of Braidwood would arise from the fact of the difference in the thickness of vein mined at Spring Valley, namely 3 feet 8 inches of coal, as compared with 2 feet 10 inches of coal at Braidwood. Now, the miners at Braidwood removed 42 inches of brushing to earn their $13.57, whereas the miners at Spring Valley only removed 16 inches of brushing to earn their $16.63. Now, as our company had to do an additional 14 inches of brushing, and, if we assume its cost to have been at the relative price paid for brushing at Braidwood — namely, 15 cents for 42 inches of brushing

—it would be equivalent to 5 cents per ton on each ton of coal mined at Spring Valley, which should be added to the 16.56 cents, to secure 30 inches of brushing, making 21.56 cents, which amount was actually paid the miners at Spring Valley in excess of what should have been paid to equalize our mining cost with that of Braidwood; and if to this we add the cost of the 12 inches additional brushing done at Braidwood, more than what was required at Spring Valley, which, at the equivalent price paid at Braidwood, amounts to 4.28 cents per ton, it would make a total equivalent of 25.84 cents more paid for mining a ton of coal at Spring Valley in 1888 than would have been paid if the price of mining at Spring Valley were on an equality with Braidwood.

To present this matter in another light: In the working places heretofore described at Braidwood 44.74 per cent. of the material moved is coal, and 55.26 per cent. is material necessary to be removed to secure 42 inches of brushing. In the same area at Spring Valley the percentage of coal produced is 59.46 per cent, and 40.54 per cent. is material removed to secure 30 inches of brushing. It will, therefore, be seen that the percentage of coal produced at Spring Valley for the same amount of labor is 14.72 per cent. greater than at Braidwood, and that it requires 14.72 per cent. less labor for brushing at Spring Valley than is required at Braidwood, and yet the cost of mining a ton of coal at Spring Valley last year exceeded the equivalent price paid at Braidwood by 25.84 cents per ton.

Assuming that the foregoing statements as to the comparative amount of labor required for a miner to mine a ton of coal at Spring Valley as compared with Braidwood are correct, and then taking into consideration the amount earned by a Braidwood miner, together with that earned by the Spring Valley miner, the amount of labor being equal at each mine, we ought to be able to arrive at what would be a fair price to the miner for mining a ton of coal at Spring Valley to make it the equivalent of the price received by the miner at Braidwood. This comparison would show that (the price now paid a Braidwood miner for mining a ton of coal being 87½ cents per ton

in a 2-feet 10-inch vein of coal, with forty-two inches of brushing) an equivalent price for mining a ton of coal at Spring
Valley in a 3-feet 8-inch vein of coal with thirty inches of brushing would be 68.14 cents per ton. The miners at Spring Valley
demand 82½ cents per ton for mining in the third vein with
sixteen inches of brushing, and, if required to do thirty inches of
brushing, then to be paid twenty cents per ton additional for the
coal mined, which would make the cost of mining a ton of coal
at Spring Valley $1.02½ per ton as compared with the price
now paid at Braidwood (where the Braidwood miner does forty-
two inches of brushing) of 87½ cents per ton.

When we come to what is known as the Streator field, we
cannot with any certainty make a relative comparison between
the Streator vein and our third vein; but our second vein of
coal and the Streator vein are similar in all respects, with the
exception that perhaps our second vein contains from five to
nine inches more coal, on an average, than the Streator vein.
We have compared, as I have stated, the Braidwood vein with
our third vein because they are similar in all respects, and both
are worked under the long-wall system. Our second vein, like
the Streator vein, is worked upon the room and pillar system.
The miners and the operators at Streator have agreed, for the
present year, upon 72½ cents per ton for mining a ton of coal,
and we are entirely willing to pay our men 72½ cents per ton
in the second vein, giving to them any advantage which this
price may give as between the Streator vein and the Spring
Valley second vein.

A word as to the alleged "pauper wages" the miners in the
Illinois coal fields have received. The statement made by the
committee of the State Board of Charities, in their report to
you, that the average monthly wages of the miners throughout
the general mining district of Illinois for the year 1888 was
$31.60, does not agree with what an average miner earned at
Spring Valley. I have had prepared a table of the work done
and the money paid to twenty-five average miners at Spring
Valley, who were permanently employed there during the last year.

I can furnish their names and further details, which would be too voluminous to embrace in this communication. A summary of this table shows that these twenty-five men, working, we believe, not to exceed seven hours in a day, mined an average of 2.7 tons of coal per day or part of a day, including 16 inches of brushing; that the average pay received by each miner for each day or part of a day worked was $2.51 per day; that, of the 298 working days in the year, the average time lost by each miner, whether voluntarily or involuntarily, was 66 days, or 22 per cent.; that the total average amount of pay received, if divided over the whole number of working days in 1888, would amount to an average of $1.96 per day for each miner, and that the total average amount paid each of these twenty-five miners for the year 1888 was $582.79, or an average of $48.56 per month for the twelve months in the year, including over two months of lost time — the amount stated being the absolute net earnings of these twenty-five men, after deducting every outlay which they are subject to.

As to the alleged profits realized by the stockholders of the company from the mining of coal, from the company's store, and from the town site of Spring Valley, they have no more foundation to stand upon than the other charges referred to herein. During the four years the work has been in operation no stockholder has received one cent return upon his invest-ment, nor will the books of the company show that he is en-titled to any. As to the company's store and its profits, I would state that, on the 1st of May last, when the mines were closed and every employé of the company had been paid what was due him in cash, the books of the store showed that there was due the store about $17,000, 85 per cent. of which was owed by the men who had been employed by the company; and this $17,000 represents not only the capital originally invested in the store, but some $4,000 over, and these debts we consider of little or no value. The total gains arising from the sale of lots at Spring Valley by the Town Site Company for a period of five years and up to this date, instead of the fabulous amount stated by certain reckless journals, will not exceed the sum of $26,000. *

---

* Statements like these, cunningly ambiguous, as careful reading will show, made without verification, and put forward by one party to a dispute for the purpose of cheapening what he wants to buy of the other — his life and labor — cannot be accepted as evidence. They are invalidated hopelessly by the demonstrations elsewhere given *ad nauseam* of the utter unreliability of all of the important statements made by the officials of the company in their various communications to the public. These allegations of loss are inconsistent with the known facts of the case. At the time of making these assertions, the president of the company had refused to accept his own offer to give up the management of his mines to his men if they would pay him a bonus of fifteen cents a ton. The company was therefore making more than that. The unprofitableness of the mines, the Town Site Company and the company store is negatived also by the eagerness of the company to resume work at wages more than double those at first offered. Nothing need be said of the evidence which could be procured of those who have seen the books and balance sheets of the various companies, and can testify that they all exhibited profits, although these may have been reinvested in the enterprise, instead of being paid out in dividends. But even if the pretense of losses was true, it does not justify one of the outrages done at Spring Valley. The Rev. John F. Power, of Spring Valley, gave the following information to a reporter of the Chicago *Inter Ocean:*

"The president of the coal company is not honest with the people. When he last met the men he made the bluff: 'Give me fifteen cents per ton royalty, and you may take the d—d mine and run it.' That was his language, and, when his superintendent offered to take the mines at the proposition, he refused to let him have them. The president says that he has lost money here. That is not true. In the last two years his mines here have netted him $160,000. The company store has netted $34,000 since it was started.

"THE COMPANY HAS MADE MONEY

on its coal operations; it has made money on its town-site investment; it has made money on its store.

"The trouble is that he has not been able to make 6 per cent. on the watered stock of $2,500,000. That is the amount of the stock they claim. It is half water. The whole outlay here cannot exceed $1,250,000. The 40,000 acres of coal was purchased to keep out competitors. They paid $10 an acre for it. That would be $400,000. The town site cost them $80 an acre. You can figure up what they are out there and for the mining machinery. I cannot see where they have invested more than $1,000,000 capital."

To which "L. W. B." of the *Inter Ocean*, after careful inquiry among the principal tradesmen and citizens, adds:

The president of the company claims he has lost money in Spring Valley. That may be, but it will take different figuring from that made by the men here to show his losses. He bought the coal under 40,000 acres of land at $10 an acre. This is an outlay of $400,000. He paid about $50,000 for the town site. He put up 200 houses at $500 each, which would represent another $100,000. This makes $650,000 of an outlay, and

LEAVES HIM NEARLY $2,000,000

of his capital stock to pay for sinking five shafts. In reality these did not with the hoisting machinery cost more than $100,000.

On the town site, which cost about $50,000, he realized more than

One of the necessary adjuncts in the operation of a property such as the Spring Valley Coal Company is tenement houses for those in the employ of the company to live in. The Spring Valley Coal Company, at an expenditure of $100,000 has constructed about 150 miners' houses. The money rent of these houses is a secondary consideration to the company, as the operation of the mines is mainly contingent upon their control and who occupies them. On the 1st of May last, when work was stopped at Spring Valley, the miners and their families then occupying the company's houses were left in possession, and they remained in undisturbed possession until about the middle of August, when the proposition of seventy-five cents per ton* was made to the men to resume work, and the superintendent of the company was instructed as follows:

"In carrying out these instructions, I desire to avoid all conflict with the men or to give them any reasonable ground for complaint; and in case any of our houses are, on receipt of this letter, occupied by the families of the men who are absent, you will not take any legal proceedings to obtain possession of such houses until the absentees have been notified, and have had time to return to Spring Valley, to remove their families. You will make no claims or demands upon the men for rents due the company since the 1st of May, unless in the case of such occupants whose ability to pay will justify you in so doing."

It is now the 25th day of September, or nearly five months (since May 1st), that many of those houses have been occupied by the men or their families, and up to the time of this writing the possession of any house has not been secured by distraint or eviction. But many of these houses are now occupied by the families of men who have left Spring Valley and are working at other mines for less wages than we are willing to pay them; others by men who will not vacate, and who have publicly

---

$300,000, making 600 per cent on his investment. The 40,000 acres of coal was purchased to keep out competition, but he has made his whole investment pay a fair per cent. on his watered stock of $2,500,000. That is what is claimed by the best business men of Spring Valley.

* Thirty-five cents a ton net.

threatened mob violence if they are disturbed in their occupancy. These men will neither work themselves nor permit others to work; and, if we should attempt lawfully to exercise a right enjoyed by every citizen of your State to regain possession of our houses by distraint (without issuing an execution or levy upon the tenants' household goods for back rents), we should expose our property to incendiarism and ourselves to the criticism of the press as oppressors of labor. If this condition of affairs is not anarchy, virtual confiscation of property, and the subordination of the law of the land to the will of the mob, then I do not know how to designate it, and yet it is apparently upheld by an intelligent and law-abiding public.

This company and its officers have been charged with closing down the mines and refusing to negotiate with the men, with the object in view of obtaining a reduced and unfair price of mining, regardless of the welfare of the men and their families. To this I answer that it is false; that I went to Chicago in April, on the invitation of a committee representing our men, to meet them there, and after I had traveled 1,000 miles to comply with their request, the committee could not travel 100 miles to meet their own engagement.

If the statements herein and the conclusions drawn from same are reliable, you, sir, and an intelligent public, will admit that the closing of our mines May 1st, last, was not for the purpose of forcing our miners to accept starvation prices for mining our coal, but that we were justified in so stopping until some fair and equitable basis for the mining of our coal could be agreed upon, based on the price paid for mining at other mines in the State where the conditions are similar.

We know of no law, moral or statute, that makes coal mining an exception, or which is not equally applicable to the conduct of any other business interest of the country; nor do we know of any moral or statute law that makes it obligatory upon the individual citizen, or a corporation, to conduct his or its business regardless of the interests of such business and the conditions of trade, solely for the object of furnishing employment to the labor of the country, when such a policy must inevitably result in the bankruptcy of the individual or corporation.

We now propose to stand on our legal, moral, and equitable rights. No amount of personal misrepresentation and abuse, emanating from a gang of professional agitators at Spring Valley and circulated throughout the country by a partisan press * can drive us or influence us to resume work at Spring Valley upon any other basis for mining than a relative price to that paid by other mines in your State, where the conditions are similar, unless we choose to do so voluntarily. And when this condition of affairs can be brought about, we are ready to start up our works, and do all within our power to find steady employment for our men.

Taking the present price of mining as agreed upon between the operators and miners at Braidwood, namely, 72½ cents per ton for mining the coal and 15 cents for 42 inches of brushing, and deducting from this the relative difference between mining a ton of coal at Braidwood and Spring Valley, on the basis of 72½ cents at Braidwood (arrived at in same manner as heretofore shown, based upon the price of 1888), of 15.07 cents per ton in favor of Spring Valley, our price for mining should be 57.43 cents per ton; and adding to the 57.43 cents the price we should pay for 30 inches of brushing, based upon the Braidwood price of 15 cents for 42 inches of brushing, namely, 10.71 cents, it would make the relative price of mining at Spring Valley 68.14 cents per ton, including 30 inches of brushing. We leave it to an impartial public to say whether in refusing to accede to the demands of the men for 82½ cents per ton, with 16 inches of brushing, and 20 cents per ton additional for 14 inches of brushing, the misrepresentations and abuse with which the officers of this company have been assailed by an unscrupulous press are justifiable.

In offering our men 75 cents† per ton for mining a ton of coal

* The severest criticisms of the company have been made by papers like the New York *World*, New York *Herald*, New York *Sun*, Chicago *Herald*, Chicago *Times*, and St. Louis *Republic*, all of which represent the party to which the president of the company belongs.

† Thirty-five cents a ton, when all the conditions of the offer were fulfilled.

in our third vein, including 30 inches of brushing, if they desired to go to work, which is 2½ cents more than is paid in the Streator field and 6.86 cents per ton more than an equivalent of the price paid in the Braidwood mines, we felt and still believe that we had made all the concessions that we can possibly make to our men and be able to maintain ourselves in a competitive market. Respectfully yours, President of the Spring Valley Coal Company, Erie, Pa., Sept. 25, 1889.

The Chicago *Times*, the only journal which printed this statement in full, commented upon it in the following editorial :

WHAT GOOD FAITH DEMANDS.

The *Times* published last Saturday a statement of the president of the Spring Valley Coal Company, addressed to the governor of Illinois, giving the company's side of the conflict with its miners.

There is one important point, which the president in his long apology passes over lightly, which deserves general attention. It is asserted that the Spring Valley Coal Company, soon after its organization, when in the process of developing its mine, offered, by advertisement and otherwise, its town lots for sale, and held out as an inducement for their purchase that the company would prosecute the business of coal-mining and make the lots offered to the public of permanent value. On these representations a very considerable number of town lots were sold, the men in the employ of the company at that time being to a large extent the purchasers. These were necessarily men of small means, and the sums which they invested, both in the purchase of the land and the construction of improvements, were to them of extreme importance. We are told that the amount invested on these representations by the Spring Valley Coal Company in lots and improvements amounted to as much in dollars as the total amount expended by the company itself in developing the mines and putting them in a condition, as the president says, for producing 4,000 tons of coal per day. The statement in regard to this important point is meager and unsatisfactory. He said: "The total gains arising from the sale of lots at Spring Valley by the Town Site Company for a period of five years and up to this date, instead of the fabulous amount stated by certain reckless journals, will not exceed the sum of $26,000."

Whether or not in the process of book-keeping the sum of $26,000 is all the profit that appears on the company's books from its town-lot operations is not of special moment. The important fact is that a large number of men of small means have been induced by the company's representations to invest their money in the purchase and improvement of real estate, and by the action of the company in closing its mines and ceasing production these lots and the improvement thereon have been rendered valueless. This is a point which the press and the public may appreciate and rightfully sit in judgment upon. If the president and his associates, who are known to be men of large means, have led poor men into losing investments by their representation, it is fair and right that they should make reimbursement for these losses.

The Spring Valley Coal Company and its owners may or may not be legally bound to make good the losses resulting from their misrepresentations in this regard. It is quite probable that the men who have invested their money in Spring Valley lots and improvements are not able to contest the matter in the courts. It is difficult to see, however, how this case differs from those in which the managers of "booms" in various parts of the country, have involved, by their misrepresentations and false statements, credulous investors. The Spring Valley Coal Company undoubtedly is composed of men thoroughly conversant with the conditions of the coal trade. They bought the property at Spring Valley knowing what miners' wages and the rates of transportation were, and on this knowledge they based their representations to the public that they could successfully conduct the coal business, and make Spring Valley a prosperous town. If they deceived themselves, as fair business men they should bear the whole loss of that deception, and not profit by the confidence which has been placed in them by men of smaller means.

There is still another view of this phase of the matter. It is for the interest of employers everywhere that laborers should be protected in the ownership of their homes. The laborer who owns his home is a better workman and a better citizen then he who lives in a tenement. The saving habit which the purchase of a home creates in the workingman is one which wise employers everywhere take pains to develop. It is a misfortune, equal to the failure of a large savings bank, when the real estate bought with workingmen's wages is made of no value. Just as the manager of a savings bank, who speculates with the hard-earned money of workingmen intrusted to him, deserves the condemnation of the press and public, so does the manager of any large enterprise who leads workingmen to invest their money in the purchase of property which he afterward, either through pique or misjudgment, destroys the value of.

If the president of the coal company would have his conduct approved by the people of Illinois, he and his associates of the Spring Valley Coal Company should take steps at once to reimburse those who have been misled into investing in the Spring Valley real estate, whether their investments have amounted to a sum which, as it is claimed, will equal the total amount of the Spring Valley Mining Company's investments in its improvements or are no more than the $26,000 which he confesses his company has profited by in its town-site speculation.

This editorial called forth the following from the spokesman of the company:

ERIE, Pa., Oct. 8. — *To the Editor :* My attention has been called to an editorial in your issue of the 2d inst., charging, inferentially if not directly, the Spring Valley Coal Company with selling town lots to residents of Spring Valley on the strength of false representations.

I should not feel justified in trespassing on your time and encroaching on your journal's valuable space if it were not tha your remarks seem to invite an explanation. They embody statements which are evidently based on a misunderstanding of the actual facts, and the inference that might be drawn from them would therefore be erroneous. ·

Unfortunately we have no literary bureau connected with our company, and consequently it would be an impossibility for us to reply to all the misstatements concerning the company published by the press of the country. If we were to undertake the task we should be obliged to give up all other business, for we should have no time to devote to anything else.

The Spring Valley Coal Company has never, so far as my knowledge goes, offered lots for sale.*

It has never, to my knowledge, disposed of any of its realty. If it has disposed of any, it must have been to such a very limited extent that it would hardly form a basis for the deceptions you seem to think the company has practiced, but which, so far as I have any knowledge on this subject, exist only in imagination.

The Spring Valley Coal Company, when it began operations, bought and is now the owner of certain real estate in the town of Spring Valley necessary for the operations of the company, present and future — if it is to be permitted by the lawless element of your State to have a future. The sale and purchase of lots at Spring Valley have been entirely private transactions, between individuals, with which the company has had nothing to do. While the parties owning the lands were to a greater or less extent interested in the company, if there has been any fraud or if false inducements were offered for the sale of lots, would it not be fairer to specify the alleged cases and let those who are personally interested answer, and not bring general or vague charges or indulge in insinuations that are supported by nothing better than idle rumors, and which are hardly worthy of refutation ?

The property-owners of Spring Valley, in my judgment, are not suffering from false representations such as your article

----

* See advertisements of the company on pages 24 and 29.

implies. If their property has depreciated in value, it is the natural result of a condition of anarchy. There is no law in Spring Valley to-day. Property rights are not recognized there, nor is the life of any man safe there after dark unless it be that of a man who is well armed and able to protect himself. No wage-worker can go to Spring Valley and exercise the rights of American citizenship and go out on the street at night without placing his life in peril.

Is it any wonder that property has declined in value at Spring Valley? What would it be worth in the city of Chicago under a similar condition of affairs? And yet high officials in your city, men who make laws as well as those whose duty it is to execute them, can find time, under the cloak of "sweet charity," to sanction the lawless condition referred to when within sight of their office windows or within one ward of your city more genuine cases of destitution and misery can be found than could be found in twenty Spring Valleys.

When law and order shall have been restored at Spring Valley, when a human life is safe there, when a property-owner can control the property that he has bought and paid for, as others control their property in your State, Spring Valley may perhaps fulfill the hopes and expectations of her citizens. But prosperity will not be secured by disregarding the obligations of law.

During the year 1888 our company paid taxes in Illinois aggregating over $8,000. This, we supposed, was our contribution for the protection of life, liberty, and property at Spring Valley. Is there not a greater principle involved in the existing condition of affairs at that place, and in which the whole people of your State have an interest, than there is in the issue which you undertake to raise. If there be any such cases of deception and misplaced confidence as you seem to think there are at Spring Valley, the aggrieved persons have the courts of law to apply to for redress, while for our company at the present time there appears to be no law except the law of the mob.

Very respectfully,
President of the Spring Valley Coal Co.

The Chicago *Times* of October 11th made this editorial rejoinder, which ended the controversy:

The president of the Spring Valley Coal Company falls into error such as Hamlet warned his mother against. He lays the flattering unction to his soul that it is the trespass of Illinois, not the soullessness of the corporation known as the Spring Valley Coal Company, that is responsible for the blight which has fallen upon the town of that name. He writes a communication to the *Times* wherein he chooses to make a distinction, into the requirements of which the *Times* does not choose to follow him, because it is practically a distinction without a difference, between the Spring Valley Coal Company and its twin brother or other close relative, the concern which has sold town lots at Spring Valley. The *Times'* position, generally stated, was that if the coal company did not propose to carry on the business of coal-mining at this place, it had no right, directly or indirectly, to sell town lots and induce settlement upon its property upon the representation that such was its purpose. Such town lots were purchased with the understanding that the industry was to be carried forward right there. He admits that "the parties owning the lands were, to a greater or less extent, interested in the company," by which he means the Spring Valley Coal Company, of which he is president. We understand how these things are done. There are wheels within wheels. The coal company buys coal lands. Certain of these lands are set aside for persons who are, to "a greater or less extent, interested in the" coal "company," and they represent, that, as here is to be a town in which will be congregated a large body of miners, we will sell this land, subdivided for the purpose as town lots. Then, in course of time, the coal company locks out the operatives upon a pretext with which the *Times* nor any humane person can have sympathy, and the town lots become next to worthless. For this depreciation the *Times* avers that the coal company, through its failure to carry

out the projects it intimated to miners and lot purchasers
it would pursue, is responsible. He says: "The property-
owners of Spring Valley, in my judgment, are not suffering
from false representations, such as your article implies. If
their property has depreciated in value, it is the natural result
of a condition of anarchy. There is no law in Spring Valley
to-day. Property rights are not recognized there, nor is the
life of any man safe there after dark, unless it be the life of a man
who is well armed and able to protect himself." Consciously
or unconsciously, he is guilty of a gross calumny not alone concerning Spring Valley, where life and property are wholly safe,
but also concerning the State of Illinois, which protects both.
He writes from Erie, Pa., and speaks without personal knowledge, or we assume he would not speak thus loosely. There
is not in all of Pennsylvania a more orderly community, nor
is there in all Pennsylvania a community more unjustly dealt
by than the settlement which the Spring Valley Coal Company induced to gather there from far and wide, and now
leaves, miners and town-site owners, and all, to the charity of
mankind.

If it was not the purpose of the Spring Valley Coal Company to carry on the business of mining at the point named,
persons more or less interested in it, of whom the president
may or may not be one, had no moral right to sell farm lands as
town lots; it had no right to gather miners from other fields
and center them there, and, when it suited the purpose of the
concern, to shut down the mines and lock out the operatives.
These Pennsylvania tactics are not welcome in Illinois. Spring
Valley is not in a condition of anarchy. It is in a condition of
extreme distress — a situation brought about not by the operatives of the mines, not by the owners of town sites, who have
good cause bitterly to repent their bargains, but by a coal company which seems to be as soulless a corporation as ever was
organized under the laws of this or any other State.

It is not creditable to the president of the company and his
associates, that they alone of all the mine-owners of Illinois,
refuse to carry forward the operations they began, and, safe in

their possession of unbounded wealth, leave poor men they had gathered about their shafts to idleness and hunger.

The foregoing statement to the public by the Spring Valley Coal Company was met by the miners with the following address to the governor of Illinois:

Hon. Joseph W. Fifer, Governor of Illinois.

SIR — The open letter addressed to you, and through you to the public, by the president of the Spring Valley Coal Company, in which he endeavors to sustain the position he has taken upon the question of mining rates for the Spring Valley field, showing, as he attempts to do, in lengthy, labored arguments, the justice and equity of his claims, based, as he presents them, upon a comparison with competitive districts, displays a willingness to meet the issue as squarely as he understands it.

In replying to his statements of the case, we must ignore a considerable portion of his letter, which has no application, so far as mining is concerned, to the present difficulty; therefore we will treat only such features as are vital to the question at issue, pointing out to you, and the public, the fallacious nature of the conclusions at which he has arrived.

It is generally understood, that, when the operators of northern Illinois offered a ten cent reduction, he made no proposition to his miners, but left them in doubt as to the terms he desired and intended to offer. When the joint meetings, brought about by the agency of the commission appointed by you, succeeded in obtaining a concession of 2½ cents, making the reduction in mining rates 7½ cents per ton as compared with last year's prices, which rates have been accepted by the miners employed in the field accepted by the strike, then it was that he proposed 75 cents for mining at Spring Valley, 30 inches of brushing, 3 men in a room, with an additional condition that in the future he would refuse to deal with his miners through their commit-

tees or as an organized body.   He says that his company " has
never asked, expected or desired a miner working in our mines
to mine coal for one cent a ton less than a fair relative price as
compared with what was paid in other fields of northern
Illinois," and intimates that they shall continue to pursue in the
future the same equitable policy that has marked their past history, yet the proposition made by him, and which he thinks fair,
and should be accepted, is a reduction of 15 cents per ton below
rates paid last year, with other conditions annexed, equal, upon
the company's own admission, to 10.75 cents per ton, as against
in the La Salle field, his nearest neighbor and competitor, of 7½
cents, with 20 inches of brushing; and the La Salle field conditions as to mining and markets are the same in every respect as
those which prevail at Spring Valley mines.

While professing a willingness to pay as much for mining as
his competitors in northern Illinois pay, he in his argument
ignores the other and more important fields surrounding him in
northern Illinois, and confines himself to a comparison of earning ability between miners employed at Spring Valley and at
Braidwood.

To show the fallacious character of his comparative reasoning,
as applied to his own and surrounding mines, let us briefly out-
line methods by which miners' wages have been and are likely
to be adjusted.

In fixing mining rates in mines shipping coal to a common
market, one of two principles must be recognized: 1st, by the
amount of labor required to produce a ton of coal, regardless
of cost of dead work, quality or ability to sell it in a competitive market; 2d, by the fixing upon a mean between the amount
of labor required to produce. The cost of production to owners and operators of mines, quality of coal and ability to compete with coals from other fields entering the same markets.

To carry out the first principle means to give a cheaper rate
of mining to miners having thick coal, which is easily mined,
and a proportionately higher rate in mines where mining is rendered more difficult through a decreased thickness of the coal-
bed and faults of other kinds that make mining hard and dis-

agreeable. Any one conversant with coal-mining knows that this method means the survival of the fittest, and is generally advocated by operators whose mines have great natural advantages in the way of thick coal and a low rate of dead work. The claims of these operators are that a day's labor is a day's labor, and whether performed in one field or the other, in a thick or in a thin vein of coal, should yield to the miner the same rate of wages per day. Upon this basis and by this method of reasoning the president of the coal company, with a view of reducing the wages of his miners, compares the earning ability of the Spring Valley and Braidwood miners. We do not believe this method, under existing conditions, is practicable, and we know, if it was applied in a general way, that it would close his mines, and his customers would purchase from more favored fields. He says that the proper relative difference between Braidwood and Spring Valley should make the price at the latter place 68.14 cents per ton. It is generally known, and cannot be questioned, that a miner in Mt. Olive mines, Macoupin County, Ill., can produce with the same labor double the quantity of coal ; and, if the equitable theory of labor cost, as urged by him, be enforced, the relative rate at Mt. Olive, as compared with Spring Valley, should be 34.7 cents per ton. This adjustment would equalize the earning power of miners and permanently close mines located and operated under similar conditions as those at Spring Valley, whereas necessity would compel miners to secure employment in more favored fields. To the miners this charge would involve temporary inconveniences, but to operators it means total loss of invested capital.

The second principle to which we referred is founded upon " a live and let live policy," by which operators and miners in a competitive field agree to share the responsibilities and divide with each other the labor and cost involved in the production of coal.

The method is the one by which all wage adjustments have been hitherto made, and, although it has sometimes given, as it must necessarily give, a greater reward to miners in thick coal than it does to miners working in thinner seams, it has also tended to keep operators nearly upon the same plane in producing and selling coal; this because it is cheaper to produce coal in a thick than in a thin vein. Hence, if a thick coal seam is profitable to operators, and if thin coal afflicted with difficulties, such as brushing, water, etc., is more expensive to operate, it cannot be questioned that it is also less remunerative to the miners, or that the disadvantages are shared by miners and operators alike.

The president of the company states, "there is not in the State of Illinois, nor in the United States, a coal property where men can work with less discomfort and greater safety to life and limb than they can in the Spring Valley mines." This is a mistake. There is as much safety at La Salle, Winona, Minonk, Bloomington, Decatur, and other places in the same coal bed, and there are dozens of larger coal fields in the United States just as safe, while, so far as comfort is concerned, Spring Valley is no better off than the places named above. All of them are free from water, yet miners in Spring Valley and other thin vein mines in northern Illinois are subjected to discomforts such as are not known in thick coal beds or in mines worked upon the room and pillar system. In the latter, miners have more space to move around freely, to stand erect and work with ease, while at Spring Valley miners work upon their knees or in a stooping position, and in loading coal must work in the narrow space left between the packing and the coal face.

Let any man who disbelieves this statement spend ten hours hard at work in a room three feet or three feet and six inches high, and convince himself that there is greater discomfort experienced than in working just as hard for the same length of time in a room five to eleven feet high.

He wants three men in a room instead of two as heretofore, and is willing to increase the length of the rooms from thirty-six to forty-two feet. The miners are willing to meet this objection by two men working in rooms forty-two feet wide, but they feel that three men working in one place often get into each other's way, and thus lessen their ability to produce.

If he does not want to cripple the earning power of his miners, and simply desires to save in roadways, he will readily grant a forty-two foot room to two men.

He also intimates that the hours of working at Spring Valley did not exceed seven. The facts are that miners at Spring Valley were compelled to be in the mine before 7 a. m. and to stay in their working places until 5 p. m., the only exceptions being when a fall of stone upon the roadway or no cars prevented them from working.

The president is evidently misinformed as to conditions at Braidwood, which he compared with those of his mines. It is true that the method of working is the same, that is to say, both places are operated upon the "long wall system." We have never heard any very serious complaints about water in the Braidwood mines, as he asserts; while some sections of the mines may at times be damp, they are not wet. If, however, he is correct in his statement that vast quantities of water accumulate at the working faces in the Braidwood mines, thereby involving additional expense for the employment of extra labor and machinery to remove it, a factor to which he attaches great importance, the owners of wet mines must be at a decided disadvantage in competing with the dry and less expensive mines at Spring Valley.

Regarding the amount of brushing done by the miners at Braidwood he has erred. He says the minimum amount is forty-two inches and the maximum four feet. There is no stipulated height for brushing required by Braidwood rules, the only requirement is that the roadway be kept four feet from the rail, and this under some conditions might necessitate three feet of brushing and under others considerably less.

There is removed by the miners two feet and ten inches of coal and from four to six inches of fire clay as mining, and to this must be added, according to him, four feet, the maximum brushing, thus making a space of over seven feet ; assuming the roof settles until it reaches the bottom, which is absurd when we consider the packing put in the place of the coal taken out, the amount of brushing would need only to be increased a few inches to cut the roadway through the solid rock.

There is a difference, too, in the manner roadways are driven, not accounted for by him as to width. At Braidwood roadways in rooms never exceed seven feet in width at the bottom, and are arched in such a manner as not to exceed four feet at the top, while at Spring Valley the requirement is nine feet at the bottom and eight feet at the top, and the labor required for this work, especially at the Spring Valley mines, by reason of the extra width and more solid nature of the strata, is even, at sixteen inches thick, almost if not equally as onerous as that performed by Braidwood miners.

The nature of the fire clay underlying the coal strata at Braidwood is more uniform than at Spring Valley. At the former place it is customary to take four to six inches of clay in mining, while at Spring Valley there is an irregular sandstone formation underlying the fire clay, which frequently touches the bottom of the coal seam, where the sandstone rock fluctuates so as to leave no fire clay between it and the coal bed, and one-third of the places at Spring Valley are affected in that manner; it then become necessary to mine in the coal, and this involves a double hardship upon the miners employed in such rooms, for which the company has allowed no compensation. It increases the difficulty of mining, and when mined and brought down, its shelly and brittle nature admits a larger percentage to pass through the screens, and for which the miner receives nothing.

We are of the opinion that if the president was more familiar with mining coal at Spring Valley than his assumptions indicate, he would not place himself in a position to be justly criticised by those who are willing to admit his superior brain power in many respects. He says: "not one additional stroke of the arm is required to bring down the coal, compared with Braidwood." Here again he errs. And it is upon errors such as we have referred to, mistakes which he accepts as facts, that the erroneous nature of his conclusions, if not the imperfection of his logic, is clearly shown. The amount of sulphur, or the number of iron bands running in the coal, determines the ease or difficulty with which it can be brought down. It is conceded that all coal contains more or less refuse, and his mines are especially cursed in this way. At Braidwood a small seam of sulphur is mostly found about the middle of the vein. This varies, as it does in all other mines, from one to two inches in thickness; in addition to this there is at Spring Valley, in nearly every place in the entire field, a band of iron pyrites two inches from the top of the seam, varying from one to several inches in thickness. There is no cleaving quality in this stone, and from six to eight inches of coal is thus lost, which diminishes materially the height of the vein represented by him. The loss of this amount of coal, however, is not the chief complaint, but the increased labor of wedging it from the stone to which it strongly adheres. Those who have had a practical experience with mining know without further comment the increased labor necessary to produce coal under such conditions.

The cost of production, whether it be due to natural disadvantages or incompetent management, does, as a matter of fact, determine the margin of profit and the prices for labor at which the mine can be successfully operated, under the head of what is commonly known as "dead work," which phrase is intended to cover operating expenses of all kinds, much of an interesting character might be furnished. In the late investigation conducted by the commission appointed by you, to effect, if possible, a peaceable and satisfactory adjustment of the mining difficulties in northern Illinois, much information of a conflicting nature was produced. This, too, from several parts of the same field, where conditions being nearly equal might reasonably be expected to illustrate this; the actual cost of dead work embracing every source of expense connected with the producing of a ton of coal at Spring Valley, which field, by reason of the absence of water and other exceptional conditions, which increase the cost of production, was, as shown by the books of that company, at the request of Messrs. Gould and Wines, the committee appointed by you, forty-six cents per ton, while the actual operating expenses of the Braidwood field, which, as the company practically admits, is higher by reason of the water and other disadvantages with which that section has to contend, disadvantages which we admit are shared to some extent equally by the miners and operators, were, as Colonel A. L. Sweet testified, equivalent to forty-five cents per ton.

Here the query naturally suggests itself, how Colonel Sweet, owning and operating mines at Streator and Braidwood, both under heavy disadvantages as compared with the dry and comparatively inexpensive mines belonging to the Spring Valley Company, paying, in addition to the extra sources of expense from which the natural conditions at Spring Valley exempt the company, five cents per ton more for all coal produced at Braidwood, could yet show, as he has done, a net expense of forty-five cents per ton against the forty-six cents in Spring Valley field, is a question that might well elicit interest and inquiry. The results here shown demonstrate one of two facts, either that the mines at Spring Valley have been under incompetent and therefore expensive management, or that Colonel Sweet's mines have been most economically conducted. If the charge of relatively increased cost is due to mismanagement or to any other cause, aside from actual and inevitable operating expenses, the great aim on the part of the company should be to remove the defects by substituting a more economical policy, instead of endeavoring to reward extravagance or put a premium upon incompetency by reducing mining rates below what is conceded to be the fair relative prices in the districts immediately surrounding him.

The miners of Spring Valley have never asked, expected or desired to receive a price for their labor in excess of a fair relative rate as compared with that paid in other fields in northern Illinois. This they believe they are entitled to, and, as the president has expressed a willingness to grant this, it only remains for him to join with his miners in an effort to arrive at the facts in the case by practical methods, such as a joint investigation as to the truth or falsity of his statements as compared to ours.

From the statements to which we have taken exception, we have proved and could, if space permitted, further demonstrate the equitable relations which Spring Valley prices and conditions, prior to the strike, gave to the miners and operators of that field as compared with those in competing districts. We have defined the advantages the Spring Valley company would enjoy as compared with other operators, and also explained the disadvantages its miners would labor under if the prices and conditions for mining at Spring Valley, as proposed, were accepted. The injustice of the president's proposition may be summed up thus: 1st. He asks his miners to do a greater amount of brushing than Braidwood miners are required to do. 2d. For this work he proposes to pay twelve and a half cents per ton less than Braidwood miners receive. 3d. He asks his miners to mine coal three feet and eight inches thick, eight inches of which is lost to the miner by reason of sulphur, and in addition thereto do the brushing above referred to at a price only two and a half cents per ton above the rate paid at Streator, where the coal is over five feet in thickness and the miners have no brushing to do. 4th. He proposes a reduction of fifteen cents per ton with thirty inches of brushing, while the original proposition at the La Salle field, his nearest competitors, operating under precisely the same conditions, and shipping coal into the same markets, was ten cents per ton below last year's rates, which proposition has since been reduced to seven and a half cents, or one half less than that demanded of us. Twenty-four inches of brushing that has by compromise been reduced to twenty inches, compared with his demand that Spring Valley miners hereafter shall take thirty inches or ten inches more in height, including extra width, than asked by his La Salle competitors.

Being willing to accept equitable conditions and prices, and to effect an honorable settlement of the present strike, we offer

1st. To work the second or thick coal vein at Spring Valley for the price paid Streator miners, namely: 72½ cents per ton; this, too, in face of the fact that the mine is yet in the crop coal, is full of faults, and up to this time has cost the company, by their own admission, over $2 per ton for mining it.

2d. Believing that the president of the coal company will admit the fact that more labor is required to mine a ton of coal in the third vein at Spring Valley than in the thick coal at Streator, we will agree to mine his thin coal for the price paid the thick coal miners at Streator, provided the company will do the brushing and building; or

3d. We will agree to an adjustment of prices and conditions such as may be determined by arbitration, or by an agreement to jointly investigate, and be governed by the facts developed by such an investigation.

Trusting that an equitable and amicable settlement may be speedily effected by some one of the methods herein submitted, we are, sir,

> Respectfully yours,
>
> PETER McCALL.
> JAMES McNULTY.
> WM. SCAIFE.
> DAVID ROSS.
> JOHN McBRIDE.

In an editorial, commenting on this correspondence between the " head " of the coal company and its " hands," the Chicago *Inter Ocean* said:

The president of the Spring Valley Coal Company complained to Governor Fifer that the press of Illinois was trying to compel him to run his mines solely in the interest of the miners. He claimed that he had been willing to pay fair wages, and he labored with an endless column of figures to show that his offer of 75 cents a ton was equal to the wages paid in other Illinois mines.

The miners in their reply do not resort to his methods of handling figures, so as to confuse rather than enlighten.   They make:

a plain proposition, which he will either accept or leave the people to infer that his first letter was not honest.

He claimed that the second or middle vein in his mine compared favorably with that at Streator. This vein is not yet developed, but the miners met him more than half way with an offer to work this vein for 72½ cents per ton, the Streator price, and 2½ cents less than the price he offered. He has claimed that every ton of coal taken from this undeveloped vein has cost him $2. He has a good chance to show the foolishness of the miners' proposition or the unfairness of his own by accepting this offer.

Another proposition from the miners seems fair. They offer to mine the coal in the third vein for the same price, 72½ cents per ton, if the company will do the brushing and road-making. This would be pay equal to that at Streator and Braidwood. Streator has no brushing to do, and the Braidwood operators pay the men 72½ cents per ton for the coal, and pay them extra for the brushing and road-making. The president of the company argued that the brushing and road making could be done for less money than his miners asked. He, in fact, offered them 2½ cents per ton for this work and sought to justify that offer in his letter to the governor. He can demonstrate this much clearer to the people of Illinois by accepting the miners' second proposition, and by building the roads and doing the brushing for 2½ cents a ton. When he has done the work and balanced his books, he may be able to show that his recent offer was fair and equitable as compared with the wages paid at Streator and Braidwood.

The miners put the president of the company in another corner by offering to submit their case to arbitration.

They have the best of the controversy so far, and will hold it unless he meets them fairly on one or all of these propositions. He cannot convince the people of Illinois that the miners are in wrong, and that he is " opposed by anarchy," by writing long letters with such statements. The fact is that he has sought to break down the miners' union in Illinois. He did not wait for a strike in his mines, he did not offer a proposition for reduced wages. He closed his mines and threw his men out of work. He kept the mines closed until after a settlement had been effected at Braidwood and Streator. Then he offered seventy-five cents a ton, the brushing to be done for nothing, and announced that he would only treat with men individually on that proposition. He would have nothing to do with any committee. In his letter to the governor, the president forgot to mention this feature of the trouble between him and his miners. It is really the one great barrier between them, and he should be manly enough to let the public see his true position, or keep quiet.

In matter and manner, the reply of the miners justifies the confident statement of President McBride at the Indianapolis convention, in December, 1889, that the men had shown themselves able to hold their own in an intellectual contest with their employers, and corroborates the manly acknowledgment of Colonel W. P. Rend, at the Columbus Joint Conference of March, 1889, that " We found they [the miners' representatives] were better equipped and better prepared with arguments than we were."